"I want to make love to you."

Ben's voice was low and husky. He leaned against his desk, feet wide apart, hands in his pockets—he looked casual, yet provocative.

"Why now?" I said, trying to control the flutters of desire in me.

"Because I've fallen in love with you, Liz."

I got up from the leather sofa, walked slowly toward him and stood close to him, in the V of his thighs.

"Do you know what love is?" he asked, wrapping his arms around me. "It's like a runaway train that won't stop and you don't know where it's going. It could kill you or . . ."

"Or what?" I said, stepping closer until I could feel his body, hard and lean against mine.

"Or it could take you to a place you never dreamed existed."

"Take me there, Ben."

"It might be a rough ride," he said.

"I'm going with you," I whispered, shaky with anticipation.

He kissed me then—slowly and languorously, but there was a hungry urgency as his mouth devoured mine, lighting fires deep inside me. And I knew wherever Ben went, I would follow. . . .

Dear Reader,

What happens to cherished, longtime friendships
when romance upsets the delicate balance and
loyalties are seen to conflict?

Frances Davies tells *you*, in her witty, incisive
style— through the eyes of Liz Crosby and Ben
Malloy. She writes about the inner struggle of a
woman who, seeking the ultimate love, risks
losing the friend of a lifetime—about the fears of a
man who, in order to conquer a woman's heart,
has to break another's.

Ben & Liz & Toni & Ross is the unique story of
four people in a tug-of-love. It is a different kind of
category romance. Obviously an Editor's Choice.

As usual, we'd enjoy hearing your comments
about this special book. Please write to us at the
address below.

The Editors

Harlequin Temptation
225 Duncan Mill Road
Don Mills, Ontario, Canada
M3B 3K9

Ben & Liz & Toni & Ross
FRANCES DAVIES

Harlequin Books

TORONTO • NEW YORK • LONDON
AMSTERDAM • PARIS • SYDNEY • HAMBURG
STOCKHOLM • ATHENS • TOKYO • MILAN

This book is dedicated to Lisa Boyes,
who imagined it;
to Joe and Robin,
for their love and generosity in Avignon;
and to Merlin,
who took it all in such good grace

Published March 1991

ISBN 0-373-25438-5

BEN & LIZ & TONI & ROSS

1

Liz

THE FIRST THING I noticed was his feet. I couldn't see the rest of him, just his feet. They poked out from behind the desk, heels splayed on the carpet, toes pointing to the ceiling.

"You in there!" I called out. "Are you all right?" Every instinct told me there would be no reply, but I called again, louder this time. "Hello?" Still nothing.

That's when I knew I'd found a body. I'd never seen a body before, and I certainly didn't want to see one now, so I was feeling more than a little desperate when I turned around and shouted down the deserted corridor, bellowing for all I was worth into the heavy Saturday silence.

"Help! Please, help! This is Elizabeth. Isn't anyone else here?"

Silence. The only sound was the burbling and humming of the watercooler.

I forced myself to cross the hall, dread dragging at my feet like mud. Politely, irrationally, I knocked twice on the half-open door before going in. The office had been unoccupied for a month; now cartons were stacked beneath the empty bookshelves.

Holding my breath I circled the desk, trying to look at him without actually seeing him, because I knew that

I was about to discover a small, neat hole in the center of his forehead. I plucked up my meager courage and managed a sidelong glance. He lay on his back, one arm flung over his head, the other at his side, like a discarded lead soldier. There was no blood. Thank God! There was no blood! I let out a long and grateful sigh. If dead men tell no tales, I thought, a publishing company is the wrong place to die.

Heart attack! Panic rose in me like a sticky sap. Heart attack I knew meant mouth-to-mouth resuscitation and beating on his chest, or something. I crouched beside him, sweating with fear. Whether he was dead or not, now I would have to touch him. It was my duty to touch him. He might still have a pulse. It was up to me to find it. Was he breathing? I held my own breath, willing his chest to move. It did move! Didn't it? Was it my imagination? With trembling fingers I touched his throat.

He was warm, very warm, and his pulse was beating slowly. Slowly and regularly. Mine raced and drummed and skipped at least nine beats at a time. He couldn't be dying, not with a pulse like that. He wasn't pale, his lips weren't blue. He wasn't anything like dead. He wasn't even passed out. He was *asleep*.

That realization sat me down hard beside him. I was panting with relief. He must be one of Paul's boozy novelists, I reasoned. He probably came in for one of Paul's notorious late-night editorial meetings and lurched into this office instead of the elevator.

"Wake up!" I said. I grabbed his shoulders and shook him, furious with him for what he'd put me through. "Wake up!"

"Ross," he muttered, without opening his eyes. "Got to go to bed...to bed, Ross...you go home...I go home. 'Night, Ross."

He rolled onto his side, flinging a heavy arm across my lap.

"Wake up!" I shook him again. "Wake up. What are you doing here? Who are you?"

He opened one eye and squinted at me as though he were trying to look into the sun, then he closed his eye and groaned.

"Shhhhh!" he whispered. "Someone is riveting deckplate to the inside of my skull."

"Who are you? Are you all right? Are you sick, or something? If you're sick you'd better tell me right now, because I'm not much good at this sort of thing. Tell me if you're sick, and I'll call an ambulance. If you're just hung over, you can fend for yourself." I have no patience with people who can't handle their liquor.

"Not sick," he finally mumbled. "Not hung over...up for three nights with a demented author. Sleep now."

"Look," I said, warming to my subject. "I don't care if you were baby-sitting Scheherazade. You scared me half to death. I came in here thinking you were dead. Really dead. Can you understand that? I've never been so frightened in my life. Look at me! Look at my hands, I'm still shaking." I held out my hands for him to see— they were shaking like palm fronds in a force-10 gale.

He opened both eyes then and gave me a long considering look. The unnerving thing was that he didn't say anything—he just looked, his black eyes flashing over me like summer lightning, and I thought of an aspen flaming like a torch. I sat there beside him with a burning flush spreading over my face and my blood singing in my ears—and I felt *singed*. Whoever he was, he had the hottest eyes I'd ever seen in my life.

"Who are you?" I repeated, and my voice sounded shaky and hoarse. "What are you doing here? Do you know where you are?"

He had closed his eyes again. "My office. This is my new office. Pomfret Press. Ross helped me move my stuff in last night. I've been with him since Wednesday. He finished his book Wednesday morning, and his girlfriend moved out on him while he was out having it photocopied. He hasn't been himself since. He's been decompressing, if you know what I mean." He yawned hugely, his eyes still closed.

"Ross? Who's Ross?"

One eye winked open, then shut, but not before he'd given me a despairing look that suggested I must be visiting New York on a ten-day package tour from Mars. "Terence Ross. Terence—author of *Blood in the Boardroom*—Ross."

No wonder he thought I was a space cadet. Terence Ross had been on the bestseller list for a hundred and fifty-three weeks. "Then you're Jack's replacement," I said lamely. "You're the new crime editor."

"Malloy," he said, propping himself up on one elbow and extending his hand. "Ben Malloy. Crime."

"Liz Crosby," I said, taking his hand. It was dry and hard and as hot as my face. "Fiction," I piped as I snatched my hand back. "If I hadn't stopped in to pick up a manuscript, I'd never have found you. This is Saturday, you know."

He nodded very, very slightly, as though he were afraid his head might fall off, and closed his eyes again. "Do you have any aspirins?"

I brought him aspirins and a glass of cold water. He tossed the aspirins back, drank the water greedily and lay down again.

"You can't sleep here," I said, recognizing the illogic even as I spoke.

"I can . . . sleep anywhere . . ." he muttered, his voice already soft and breathy and full of sleep. ". . . floor . . . deck . . . foxhole . . . jail . . . slept in a tree once . . . slept in a cave . . . dark cave . . . trickling water . . . tickling, trickling waters of . . ." Then he fell away from me into a tunnel of sleep.

Gently, I loosened the glass from his relaxed fingers, and surveyed the rest of him. When vertical he would surely be tall. He wore jeans, ancient salt-bleached deck shoes without socks and a faded blue T-shirt with the silhouette of a fish embroidered above the pocket. Beneath the fish was the legend Sausalito Baits.

His hair was absolutely sensational. It was black— not ordinary black, but blue-black, which has always been my favorite color for a man's hair. And it was absurdly thick and curly, with the lightest possible dusting of gray just above the ears. If there's anything that sends my hormones racing around like bumper cars it's blue-black hair with a touch of frost at the temples. His eyebrows were straight, and his nose had a not unattractive bump on it. Someone, somewhere, must have connected with it. I suppose it's an occupational hazard, but I couldn't help thinking what a perfect dust jacket photo he'd make. In an open-throated shirt with a tweed jacket slung casually over his shoulders, he would have been ideal for *Hour of the Cougar*, our international spy thriller, the author of which was actually a chinless, bug-eyed New England recluse. I was picturing Malloy in an Aran sweater with a pipe clamped between his teeth when his eyes flew open and his black eyes flashed. I jumped up guiltily.

"She was every detective's dream," he said, looking right through me and speaking in the slightly artificial voice of someone quoting. "She was tall, she was blond, she was sexy, she was trouble." Then his eyes banged shut.

I found his jacket on a chair, covered him with it and closed the door.

"TONI? TONI, are you up?" I closed the apartment door behind me. "I'm home. You're never going to believe . . . Toni?"

Toni's rich, but ragged mezzo-soprano soared above the drumming of the shower. "Ya-ha-ha-hoo-ha-ha-ha-hee!" She always did scales in the shower.

I tapped on the bathroom door and walked into a wall of fragrant steam, saying, "It's me. You just get up? Wait till I tell you what—"

Toni shrieked, "Shut the door! It's freezing. I'll be out in a sec."

"Don't shut off the water. I'm all sweaty." I peeled off my clothes and dropped them in the hamper.

Toni, cooked to the color of a boiled prawn, stepped dripping from behind the shower curtain. Toni was generously built—along the lines of her idol, opera singer Marilyn Horne—but she always hooked up with thin, ungenerous men. Her boyfriend then was always telling her how much he admired particular women. These women were invariably thin.

"Quick," she said, one hand on the shower curtain, "get in before we have water all over the floor." We exchanged places in an accomplished adagio we'd had years to perfect. As college roommates thrown together by the whim of the dormitory assignment computer, we'd taken to each other from the first afternoon, not because we were alike, though we were in many ways, but because in so many other ways we were utterly different. Discovering each other was like finding a whole new, if oddly familiar, species.

That had been seventeen years ago, when we were both eighteen. Sometimes it seemed like a lifetime ago, sometimes it felt like the day before yesterday.

I REMEMBER—I had no sooner dragged my shiny freshman suitcases into the dorm sitting room I was supposed to share for the next four years, when this redheaded dumpling with a camera in front of her face bounced off the sofa and carommed around the room like a loose tennis ball, all the while snapping pictures of me like a maniac. As suddenly as she started, she stopped.

"Hi! You must be Crosby, E. I'm Durance, A. The *A*'s for Antoinette, but everyone calls me Toni. Would you mind coming in again? I'm shooting a feature for the campus paper. Freshman Orientation: The Trauma of Arrival. I'd like another couple of shots—just for insurance."

"Why me?"

"You look like a typical, average freshman."

I didn't feel at all typical. In fact I felt quite singular. "How did you manage to get an assignment from the paper already?"

"I walked into the office, showed them some of my pictures and suggested the story. They fell all over themselves. It's a dumb paper, but it's good experience."

"What are you majoring in—salesmanship?"

"Art. I picked up a couple of maps of the campus, and pumped a sampling of upperclassmen for the straight scoop on which are the gut courses and which are worth going to, and I've found out which bars in town don't bother to ask for an ID."

I was dazzled.

"C'mon," said Toni. "Be a good sport and go out and come in again. Just once?"

Before the afternoon was over, I must have gone out and come in that door about fifty times. Then we went out for pizza and started to talk. We talked about growing up. We talked about school. We talked about boys. But mostly we talked about Life. With a capital *L*. We wanted so much, and we were sure we'd figure out how to get it. Get it all, without any crummy compromises. Toni was going to be a painter. I was going to do something with English literature, maybe teach. We would both be famous.

We talked all night, that first night—it's something we still do, even after seventeen years of being closer than close. Over the years we have sustained each other through thick and quite a lot of thin—lost jobs, failed love affairs, biopsies, root canals. In all that time, there has been no awfulness that either of us has had to meet alone.

HOT WATER POURED OVER ME, loosening the knot of tension between my shoulder blades. I thought about Ben Malloy and hummed a little to myself.

"Where have you hidden the hair dryer?" Toni asked.

This was a mock-serious, if constant question. "Where have you hidden the olives...the laundry tickets...my portfolio..." We had been sharing an apartment for nearly two years, and Toni still pretended that my dislike of rigid systems is either a congenital defect, or some sort of devious plot to subvert the natural order which it is her mission to impose upon my unruly world.

"On the back of the door," I said, "under my robe."

The blow-dryer roared to life, and I deferred telling Toni about Malloy until I had a chance to put my thoughts in order. I soaped my arms and tried to tell myself he was nothing special, but I didn't believe it for a minute. New York may be full of men like Ben Malloy who look like Ralph Lauren ads, but none of them stared at me with Ben's hot black eyes.

When I finished my shower I found Toni in the kitchen, blow-drying the polish on her toenails. "Your choice," she said, "salad or veggie omelet?"

"Veggie omelet." Toni's veggie omelets hinted at divinity.

She rummaged through the fridge. "How about sautéed shallots with red Holland peppers and cubed feta?"

"Be still my heart," I murmured. "Hand me the eggs." She really is the world's greatest short-order cook. "You're not going to believe—" I began as I broke eggs into a bowl, "—you'll never guess what I found at the office this morning. It's too bizarre."

"Try me,' she said. "After the week I've put in, I'm ready to believe anything." She sat across from me at the kitchen table, carefully slicing a pepper along its seams.

I told her about discovering Malloy, and even before I came to the part about him talking in his sleep—if he actually was talking in his sleep—she stopped peeling.

"You're making this up," she said. "You're trying out some writer's plot on me."

"It's true, I swear. Cross my heart and hope to die. You're bound to meet him at the office in the next couple of days." Toni was our art director at Pomfret Press. "If he's not the most gorgeous thing since Cary Grant played Whatshisname in *Notorious*—"

"Devlin. He can't be that good-looking."

"But he is that good-looking."

"Then he's either already involved with someone, or there's something terribly wrong with him. He's probably married, or he's got a drinking problem, or he beats up little old ladies, or he's into *S* and *M*. Why would such a good-looking guy be running around loose?"

"I really don't think he's involved. A man involved with one woman just doesn't look at another woman the way he looked at me. You know what I mean? Just the way Devlin looked at Ingrid Bergman."

"Alicia Huberman," amended Toni, who has an old-movie memory like a video rental catalog of golden oldies. She shook her head at me and laughed what I called Toni's "French laugh." Very sharp and staccato. "Hawn! Hawn! Hawn!" It was a discouragingly cynical laugh.

I tried to explain—which was difficult, because it wasn't at all clear to me. "I'm not sure, exactly, what it is about him. I don't know, maybe it's his eyes. Did I tell you he has the most astonishing black eyes? I mean they're huge, and when he looks at me . . ."

"When he looks at you, what?"

"Well, they do something to me. Right here." I patted my middle. "I know it's crazy. But everything inside sort of melts..."

"Here we go, kids!" she whooped.

"You're jumping to conclusions."

"It's been two years since Michael."

"Don't remind me."

"Two years is a long time to go without a man."

"What would you know about it? You've got Ned."

"I know that you're glowing. Yes, you are. Glowing."

"Nonsense." But I could feel the flush in my cheeks. I whisked the eggs furiously.

When all the peppers were peeled, she said, "Do you remember Wanda Ridgeway—Wanda Byland, that was?"

The name meant nothing to me.

She pushed the cutting board with its peppers across the table to me. "Chop," she said. "Think back. Wanda was the oboe player who lived one floor down when we were in school. She went to the music library one night and discovered this humpy law student in the stacks. He was fast asleep on one of the shelves. He'd taken all the scores down and gone to sleep. It was just like *Sleeping Beauty.* In reverse, of course. Naturally, they fell madly in love..."

"And lived happily ever after, I suppose."

"I have my doubts. He's a scandalously rich tax attorney in Mill Valley and probably the most boring man. So beware of Sleeping Princes, Lizzie. I don't think they're made for the long haul." She passed me a couple of shallots. "Mince," she said.

"How do you know all this?" I was always astonished by the breadth of information Toni still accumulated about college acquaintances I'd long since forgotten. I wondered sometimes if she was afraid to let them go.

"I ran into them a couple of years ago at San Francisco Opera. I was supposed to be at a book designers' convention, but Jackie was singing 'Adalgisa' to Joan's 'Norma', so of course..." Her shoulders scrunched up to her ears and just as suddenly dropped. This was Toni's "French shrug." It said: Who in his right mind could argue with such a decision?

She called Marilyn Horne "Jackie" and Joan Sutherland "Joan." She'd never met either one. This is one of the parts of being an opera lover that I do not understand. Agatha Christie has been universally adored since my great-grandmother was an infant, but no one has ever said, "I see there's a new Agatha in all the book stores."

Toni turned from the stove to wave her wooden spoon at me. "There's something about that name, Ben Malloy, that's familiar."

"Not to me."

She tipped the omelet pan thoughtfully, then turned back to me. "I wonder if he could be the same Malloy who wrote that Vietnam novel. I did a dust jacket for a Ben Malloy novel when I first started, a thousand years ago, at Pyeman and Wooster..."

"I don't know, I've never heard of him."

"...It must have been fifteen years ago."

We ate our omelet and discussed what to get our friends Sandra and Bill for wedding presents. Toni was thinking about going down to SoHo to that shop that sells hand-carved dough-bowls.

I tried to be reasonable. "Sandra only goes into the kitchen when she needs ice. What on earth would they do with a hand-carved dough-bowl?"

"What most people do with a dough-bowl—set it on a table in the foyer and toss mail into it."

"I was going to send shrimp forks."

"You always send shrimp forks."

"Just a minute," I said. "Let me do a little calculation." I closed my eyes and counted. When I came to the end of the list I said, "In the past two years we have bought, between us, wedding presents for eight friends—that does not include business acquaintances or the secretarial pool."

Toni nodded gloomily. "Did you count Phyllis and Canute? If you forgot them, it's nine."

"Nine, then."

"Does it really bother you that much that everyone seems to be getting married? Or at least pairing up?"

"I thought living with Michael had cured me. Breaking up with him was like an inoculation against commitment. But lately I've begun to wonder if I'm really going to be satisfied to end my days as Crosby, E., spinster of this parish."

"There are worse things, you know. You could be married to someone as boring as Wanda's tax attorney. Besides," she added, laughing, "you can't move out on me now, not when we've finally gotten our periods back in sync again."

It was true. We were in sync again, just like in our college days.

"Rob and Jeanine called this morning," Toni said. "They said the wind is terrible. Madame Agougou next-door swears it was the wind that blew her new blue Citroën into Jeanine's rosebushes. Jeanine, of course, believes the worst."

Toni's French cousins lived in the south of France, in Avignon. He was an ophthalmologist and she worked in a bank. Every August they fled the heat of Avignon for the Swiss Alps, while we, who adore the heat, took over their house for a month. We'd gone there three years running and planned to go on doing so as long as *les cousins* were willing to let us use the house. Let others troop off to the Hamptons, to Fire Island, the Cape, and Martha's Vineyard, where they will invariably find themselves spending their summer vacation talking to all the same people they talk to every day back in New York. Not Toni and me. Avignon was the lodestar by which we steered through each year's storms. Avignon held out the blissful promise of one month of perfect peace and perfect privacy. A place where the garden walls were high enough to allow us to skinny-dip at any hour, and we could alternate swimming lazy laps in the turquoise pool with baking on the terrace in the blazing Provençal sun. But August was still months away. This was early April, Avignon's season of scouring winds and blossoming pear trees.

"Do you want to ask anyone along?" Toni said.

"Gosh, no. Even if I wanted to, who is there for me to ask? Are you asking Ned?"

"He's working."

For the past five years, or so, Toni had been having a vague sort of on-again off-again affair with an actor. He had a very small role on a TV soap opera. "Daytime serial" was the term he preferred. Toni suspected he was trying to build this into a much larger, more telling role, by sleeping with the show's lady producer. He was often stopped on the street by women who recognized him as Dr. Jack Jilson, the alcoholic hematologist on *Metropolitan Medical Center*. Toni said they admired his profile almost as much as he did. I think that's the reason she was drawn to him in the first place—his profile. It was straight out of a Caravaggio painting, as she never tired of pointing out to me in the early days of their romance. All those years she spent in art history conspired to make him irresistible.

"Look," I said, hoping to get her mind off Ned. "What about lace? How do you think Sandra feels about Battenberg lace?"

2

Ben

I'VE NEVER BEEN a man to talk in my sleep, but I woke
to the sound of my own voice. I was groaning. If you
want to know what misery is, try sleeping on your office floor. I've snoozed in shell holes that were more
hospitable. It was dark when I woke up, and I felt as
though I'd gone fifteen rounds with a boxing kanga-
roo. My jacket was crumpled under me—a small mystery, because I thought I remembered dropping it onto
a chair, but in all honesty, my recollection of Friday
night was not what you might call overly detailed. I
only knew I was in my new office and that my mouth
tasted like the inside of a welder's glove. Cold water was
what I needed, and a shower, and food. I struggled to
my feet, my knees cracking like sidearm fire.

At the watercooler, I drank a dozen elf-sized cups of
water. The water reminded me of something or someone I had dreamed about, but I couldn't call it back. All
the way down in the elevator I worried at the dream,
tried to grab hold of it, tease it out, but it was no good.

It was a typical spring night in Manhattan. A dank
breeze off the East River blew ragged scraps of mist
across Madison Avenue. What passes for air these day
in midtown was sharp with the hellfire smell of diesel
exhaust. I grabbed a cab and went home. I showered,

ate two cans of beef stew and four slices of toast, washed it all down with a quart of buttermilk, and fell into bed feeling clean and full.

It was just as I was teetering on the lip of sleep that I remembered the girl. Fair as wheat, wide-eyed, frightened. Was she part of my dream? Why was she frightened? I was still trying to break through the haze of that memory when I slid into a dream pulling her in after me....

ROSS AND I HAD a standing date for Sunday breakfast. We met at Mona's Acapulco. We liked Mona's because it was the only café on Columbus Avenue that didn't serve brunch. It was dark and scruffy. There was no track lighting, no ferns, no waiters on roller skates. It had no ambiance, unless you call flyspecked bullfight posters and faded serapes ambiance. We always ordered the same thing: huevos rancheros, rice and beans, and Mexican beer, which we drank from the bottle.

Ross still looked scorched around the edges, but at least he'd lost that awful startled look of a man who's just taken a bullet in the back. When you've known someone as long as I've known Ross, you know when he needs to talk and when it would be better to say nothing. Ross was putting away his breakfast with theatrical zest. From the way he ate you'd think he'd just discovered salsa.

"Let me tell you about the Jerk..." he began. "The Jerk" was his shorthand for Jeremy Bevis, the photographer his girlfriend Iris—a fashion model with the mental agility of a snow pea—had run off with. Why he mourned for her, I'll never understand. Any woman who would run out on a guy on the same day that he finishes a book he's worked on for two years is about as generous-spirited as a Portuguese man-of-war. But I know that when your friends are in love, it's hopeless to expect them to act rationally. And when they're falling out of love, or getting over love, they're more irrational than ever.

He must have decided not to tell me about the Jerk, because the next thing he said was, "I miss her, Ben. I can't help it."

I made sympathetic noises, and we ate for a while in silence.

"Do you know anything about jade plants?" said Ross.

I reached over and cuffed him on the shoulder. "C'mon, buddy. You know the only thing I know how to grow is hair." It was an old joke between us, not the kind you laugh at, but the kind you repeat because it's so old and tired it makes you both feel better.

"She didn't even take her jade plant. How does she expect me to water the thing when I don't know how often?"

"She doesn't expect you to water it, Ross. She expects you to let it die."

"I can't let it die," he protested, his eyes brimming.

"Give it away."

"I can't."

My heart damn near broke for him when he said that. I knew better than to say something like, "C'mon Ross, she's not worth it." He was still so in love with Iris he would have probably hauled off and punched me in the nose. Again.

Ross and I had been buddies since the night he broke my nose. He wasn't my author then—I knew him only casually. He was edited by a guy down the hall. We ran into each other one night in a bar. Since I didn't want to talk about his books, I started talking about the Mets. Then he told me how much he respected my opinion and asked me point-blank if I liked his books. He'd published two, and I knew from his editor that he was having trouble with his third, *Bloody Thursday*.

Because very few writers want the truth, I stalled, trying to decide if Ross was one of the rare ones who could handle it. I told every anecdote I'd ever heard or read about Dashiell Hammett. I threw in some about Graham Greene. When I finally ran out of anecdotes I thought to hell with it and told him I didn't much like his books. I told him I thought they were phony. I told him he was trying too hard to be Elmore Leonard.

That's when he punched me in the nose. I popped him on the chin so hard that he bit a chunk from his lower lip. The bartender hustled us both out onto the sidewalk, so we sat on the curb, with the blood running down our chins, and Ross, who looks as if he should be playing defensive end for the New York Giants, cried. He laid his big shaggy head on my chest and he wept like a little kid. Then he told me the book he was working on was pure garbage. He said he was paralyzed with fear because he didn't know how to fix it.

We went over to his place then and opened a couple of beers and started to talk, really talk. And before we knew it the sun was coming up. We had told each other all about our wars and our writing and our women, and what we told each other was the truth. Most of it, anyway.

I took his manuscript home with me and a couple of nights later we met again. We talked all night that second night, too, but this time we talked about how to fix his book. I've been his editor and best friend ever since.

ROSS, WITH HIS HEAD bent to his plate, continued eating with exaggerated concentration, his big jaws bulging as he chewed. When he looked up I could tell from his eyes that the fire-storm was over. At least for now.

"Tomorrow's your big day," he said finally, mopping up salsa with a rolled tortilla. "You're going to be new kid on the block all over again. New job, new faces. I hope you're planning to stay put for a while. I'm not crazy about switching publishers so often. This is the second time in five years, you know. It makes me nervous, Beniamino."

Ross pretended to believe, because I have black hair and eyes, that I was Sicilian and connected to the Mob. He said my name was really Beniamino Malatesta, and that I had been swiped from my cradle by Irish tinkers.

"If it makes you nervous," I said, "you shouldn't have opted to come with me."

"C'mon. What choice do I have? We've been a team since *Bloody Thursday.* 'Wither thou goest . . .' and all that. You want another beer?" Ross sat back and sucked a tooth. "We're both getting too old for this game of musical desks you've been playing. I wish you'd settle into a publisher and stay put for a while. Like maybe the next twenty years."

The waitress brought two more beers and we both watched her hips as she walked away with our plates. "Isn't she something?" said Ross. In silent tribute we raised our bottles and toasted her hips.

I took his appreciation to be a sign of returning mental health.

"Do you ever wonder where the time goes?" I said. "One day you're clipping a Ted Williams card against your bike spokes, and the next day the world is full of girls. They're everywhere. Like they all sprang up overnight after a spring rain. Like daisies."

"When I was a kid," he said, "all I thought about was baseball and girls and getting out of high school so that I could go to college."

"And they all smelled so good," I said.

"I was sure that everything I didn't understand would be made clear as soon as I took my first class. I thought it would be like a transfusion—they'd pump it all into me. The tough stuff like Henry James and molecular oxidation and Plato. But somehow biology and philosophy kept being shoved aside. And all I thought about was getting laid, and reading novels, and writing novels."

"Like flowers," I said. "They smelled like flowers."

"Then I went into the army and all I thought about was getting laid and not getting killed."

"Real flowers, not the stuff that comes out of bottles. And rain. All the girls smelled of rain and cotton shirts that have dried in the sun."

Ross groaned. "And they all wore those cute little cotton underpants. You know what I am? I'm what the demographers call a mature adult. I've been to college and I've been to war. I've written a bunch of novels, my girl's walked out, my hairline's receding, and I haven't changed since I was sixteen. I'm still obsessed with books and getting laid."

"I don't think it ever changes," I said. "I wouldn't tell anyone else this, Ross, but I've been having the most fantastic dreams."

"Yeah?"

"Always the same woman. Over and over all last night. Dream about her. Wake up. Dream about her. Wake up."

"Who is she?"

"That's just it. I don't know. But I don't think I'm making her up. I think she's real. She's someone I've actually met somewhere. But I can't remember where, and it's driving me crazy."

"Dreams are just dreams, Ben." He sounded so wistful I thought he was going to segue back to Iris, but just then the waitress brought the check, and Ross grinned up into her eyes and said, "Do you know anything about jade plants?"

3

Liz

"MISS CROSBY?"

I had just started on a particularly difficult revision letter when Hadley Pomfret knocked on my door. I hoped that if I didn't answer he might, being a shy man, lose heart and go away.

The company for which we worked, Pomfret Press, was small. It was privately held. Hadley Pomfret owned it jointly with his brother Harold. They'd inherited it from their father, who'd inherited it from his father before him. Though we preferred to think of it as cozily shabby, it had long ago crossed the line into scruffiness. This was by design, for Hadley Pomfret lived in terror of the day when Harold—who cheerfully collected his codirector's salary, but could be counted on to visit the office only for the Christmas party, and had never once asked to see a year-end statement—discovered that Pomfret Press was far more profitable than its grungy premises suggested and therefore ripe for takeover. Hadley was determined to keep Pomfret Press from being gobbled up by the conglomerate barracudas. Books to him were still books, not products.

It was for this reason that the staff of Pomfret Press were better paid than most, and therefore expected not to complain about asylum-green walls in the corridors, a telephone system that was little better than soup cans linked by string, and pull-chain cistern lavatories that would shame even an emerging nation. It was our collective assumption that the Pomfrets owned the building, though no one had ever actually seen the deed.

All the editorial offices were on one floor. On the floor below were publicity and the art department where Toni, as art director, ran the show. It was her department that designed the books, their jackets, and their advertising.

Softly, Pomfret rapped again.

I wanted to finish my letter. If you really care about your authors, and most editors do, revisions letters are always ticklish things to get right: no matter how much we might praise a book in the first paragraphs, the author will invariably interpret any suggestions for improvements and rewrites as terminal diagnoses.

I sat with my hands poised above the typewriter keys, waiting, willing Pomfret to go away.

He knocked again. "Miss Crosby?" Mr. Pomfret never used our given names; that degree of informality was generally reserved for secretaries and typists.

"Come!" I called, giving up.

Pomfret hesitated in the doorway. "Sorry," I lied. "I was on the phone."

Gudrun, my secretary-assassin appeared beside him, gazing down at him with the moist, obedient eyes of a King Charles spaniel. The eyes she turned on me were as flat and cold as glass. I shared Gudrun with three other editors, all men. She planned to have my job on a plate within five years.

Gudrun was nine feet tall, flaxen-haired, and looked like a super model. She spent her lunch hour swimming laps at the West Side Y where, I'd been told, she did not tap the toes of a swimmer she wanted to pass, but bit them. I believe this to be true.

"Could you," began Pomfret, "spare Gudrun? I'd like her to give our new editor a tour of the house."

There was no way in hell I was going to turn this woman loose on Ben Malloy. Not when I planned to turn *myself* loose on him.

"I really would like to," I said, improvising furiously. "Nothing would please me more, but it's imperative that Gudrun dig up the manuscript I was working on last Friday. It seems to have grown legs and walked off somewhere."

Gudrun gave me a look that would have fried the eyeballs of a lesser woman.

"Not to worry," I said blithely. "I'd be delighted to do it myself. I'll give Mr. Malloy the standard house tour."

"You know him then?" said Pomfret.

"Indeed," I replied.

"Too kind," murmured Pomfret. "Too kind."

WHEN I WALKED INTO his office, Malloy's mouth fell open and he positively leaped out of his chair.

"You're real," he said when he finally found his voice. "I thought you were a part of my dream. I thought—"

"Liz Crosby," I said. "I didn't suppose you'd remember—"

"Remember? I've done nothing but remember ever since Saturday, but I thought I'd made you up. Like Xanadu. Would you like coffee? There's a ten-foot teutonic creature out there who's quivering to minister to my every need."

I declined his offer of coffee with my very best regretful smile. "I'm here to take you on the official Pomfret Press office tour."

"That's very kind of you." His words were formal, but his eyes twinkled and glittered.

"My pleasure," I said, all but purring.

I'd like to be able to say I took him from one editor's office to another, introducing him with wit and grace, but I was so hyperconscious of him, that most of what I remember is about as scintillating as, "Jim, Ben. Ben, Jim." It took all my concentration to put one foot in front of the other and make it down the hall. Eventually he met the whole editorial crew. I even pointed out Mr. Grice who was scurrying around a corner in his beetle-brown suit. Like the White Rabbit, he was always in the most tremendous hurry. "Time is money. Time is money," was his rallying cry. Mr. Pomfret, I explained to Ben, had finally decided to join the twentieth century and put all the Press's records on computer discs. It was Mr. Grice's job to do this. He was an accountant who specialized in what he called "client-friendly" programs. God help us!

Where Gudrun's tour would probably have ended with Ben Malloy backed up against the shelves in the supply room, my tour concluded at Toni's office in the art department. I'd be less than honest if I didn't admit that I was relieved when I introduced them and they seemed to hit it off immediately.

Then Toni said, "I designed a book by a Ben Malloy when I was at Pyeman and Wooster. I was wondering if you—"

"The blame is all mine, I'm afraid." His smile was graciousness itself, but his eyes said, *This is not something I want to talk about.*

"You must know Bill Byrne," I put in hastily.

"You know him, too?" Ben said, instantly more at ease.

Toni poured us coffee from her pot and the three of us chatted about publishing people we knew in common. From time to time I caught Toni's eye—it was plain to me that she seemed to like him.

Ben and I climbed the stairs back up to our floor. One of my authors claims to have completed his novel while waiting for our elevator. Ben stopped on the landing.

"What's that scent you're wearing?"

"*Pluie de printemps.*"

"Pardon?"

"Spring rain."

For some reason he grinned so widely he looked about nineteen. "Have lunch with me."

I like a man who's forthright and direct, so the invitation was a point in his favor, but I couldn't do it. "I'm sorry, I'd really like to, but I'm lunching with an agent." This was not a date I could possibly break. The agent had a book I desperately wanted for my list.

"Then let's make it dinner. Are you free for dinner?"

"I'd like that very much."

Gudrun chose that moment to come crashing through the stairwell door on her way to share her morning noggin of fruit juice and lecithin with Lars in the mail room.

"I found it!" she said. "I found your wandering script."

"Where was it?"

"In your bookcase, beneath a pile of stuff."

"But that's impossible. I'm positive I left it on my desk. How would it get in the bookcase?"

Gudrun shrugged. Not wanting her to think I blamed her for its disappearance I said, "Well, it doesn't matter, as long as it's turned up." How wrong I was to think it didn't matter.

Gudrun sniffed. "That's the good news. The bad news is that the last three chapters are missing."

"Then keep looking. They must be somewhere." Suddenly, I shivered. It was the same shiver you get when a goose walks over your grave.

Gudrun huffed down the stairs, and Ben and I fled up the stairs to our respective offices. I, of course, called Toni instantly. "I gather you liked him," I said.

"Wow! If he were blond, I'd give you a run for your money."

"You wouldn't!" I knew she wouldn't. Of course she wouldn't. Loyalty is Toni's longest suit.

EAGER THOUGH I WAS to dash off to dinner with Ben, I couldn't leave the office until I'd met with Mr. Pomfret to discuss the acquisition of Gillian Ypes's latest book, *The Ladies at Sunset.* I had spent three hours over lunch dickering with her agent, but no book was ever bought without Mr. P.'s approval—it was his money after all. But, as much as he loved books, our Mr. P. was not overly fond of Gillian Ypes. In his more forthcoming moments he would concede that he didn't really understand her, but he had to admit she did sell—and more than modestly. Her following, I'd been trying to convince him, was growing.

Six o'clock was when my delicate negotiations with Mr. Pomfret began, negotiations too delicate to be interrupted by personal phone calls along the lines of, "I may be rather late, I'm afraid. Please wait." I tried to put Ben out of my mind and concentrate on selling Mr. P. on Gillian Ypes on the basis of three chapters and a synopsis.

It was nearly nine o'clock when I left Pomfret, his approval finally won. I was prepared to discover that Ben had given up and left, but I found him in his office up to his ears in manuscripts. I doubt he even knew how late I was.

"Hungry?" he said.

"Starved."

"Where do you want to go?"

"I don't know. Where do you want to go?"

Even as we spoke, this same tedious colloquy was being repeated by thousands if not millions of couples all over New York. The very idea gave me a headache. Next would come the litany of choices: Austrian? Bavarian? Chinese? Danish? Ethiopian? French? Greek? Haitian? Italian?

"Italian," I said.

"There's a great little place right in my neighborhood."

"Where do you live?" I said, trying not to sound as though I were angling for an invitation, which I wasn't. One is curious, after all. It's only natural.

"West side," he said. "Near Lincoln Center."

"So do I." We were so pleased with ourselves at this revelation we positively smirked at each other as we headed for the elevator.

Every once in a while, almost as though someone had sprinkled fairy dust over the city, I would step out of a building onto the sidewalk to discover everything had been transformed. The air was almost fresh, as though blown into midtown by a cosmic fan in Central Park— you could smell trees and newly mown grass. The buildings sparkled, all the lights twinkled as if equipped with star-filters, the evening sky was as clear and blue as the dust jacket on a Big Sky novel. It was promise. Everything was bursting with promise. I knew this as I walked uptown beside Ben Malloy.

I tried to tell myself that this sudden euphoria would pass, that it was nothing but a bunch of hormones colliding with expectation, but just at that moment Ben put his hand beneath my elbow to steer me between a couple of vengeful taxis, and I swear my feet left the ground and I floated across the street. If I hadn't been carrying a briefcase full of scripts I would have floated clear away.

As we walked we chatted about restaurants in what we had now agreed was Our Neighborhood and which ones we liked best, but we weren't talking about restaurants at all. It's hard for anyone who's not in what I now recognize as the first stages of falling in love to understand how much subtext we managed to get out of, "Do you like Fettucini Bettina?" On the other hand, if you are falling in love, or remember what it was like, you'll know exactly what I mean when I say that I very nearly came apart when Ben said, "Take oysters. Don't you think there's something particularly sensuous about eating raw oysters?"

That evening with Ben was not like any other first date I've ever had. Everyone knows what happens on first dates. The first date is the one where two people condemn themselves to sit nervously in a restaurant, their hearts at once brimming with hope and constricted with dread, while they lie to each other about how much they really, really like the symphony, or goat cheese, or art deco.

As soon as we had ordered dinner and a bottle of wine Ben said, "Are you...um...going with anyone?"

As he spoke his eyes were huge. I didn't have to be clairvoyant to read his mind. What he was really saying was, *Life's too short for all the games other people play to hide their nakedness from each other. I like you, Elizabeth. I'd like to go to bed with you.*

I smiled at him and sipped some wine. "I'm not attached, no." My eyes said, *I like you too, but don't rush me,* and from the way he smiled back I knew he read me perfectly.

We talked easily after that. About books, mainly, and authors. What else would editors talk about? Heads together over coffee and liqueur, we gossiped shamelessly, offering each other scandalous stories, like succulent after-dinner tidbits.

It was Ben who finally changed the subject. He said, "I couldn't help noticing you and Toni sending silent signals over your coffee cups. You're pretty close, aren't you, you two?"

"Always have been. Since our first year in college. Toni's my best friend. We live together." I was surprised at how defensive I sounded.

"Really?" he said. "How come? I would have thought you'd cramp each other's style."

I saw that at that moment I had a choice: I could tell Ben the truth, or I could fob him off with some plausible explanation.

Considering my answer forced me to ask myself exactly how interested I was in this man. Every woman knows there are stages in a relationship when you tell a man the absolute, pure, unvarnished truth, so-help-you-God. On the other hand, a woman would have to be a fool not to know that there are other times when the truth you tell is not an absolute truth, but a modified or edited truth. Is there a woman alive who, when asked after the first time, *Was it wonderful for you, too?* has answered, *No?*

Where truth was concerned, Toni and I operated on the same premise. With each other, we were scrupulously honest; we told each other everything. With the men in our lives, truth was on what you might call a need-to-know basis.

THE REAL TRUTH was that it all began when the turkey fell on my foot.

Michael—my ex-boyfriend—and I had just left one of those Sunday brunches where the men take themselves off to the den, and according to the ancient and beloved rituals of their tribe, spend the best part of the afternoon watching footfall on the television. Meanwhile, we women, abandoned, indulged ourselves in such riveting topics as the effect of Bonn's new economic policy on the World Monetary Fund, and whether people who cry on Barbara Walters's show are sincere.

The game over, the place cleared like a fire drill.

"Hurry up, Liz," Michael pleaded, jabbing at the elevator button. "I don't want to miss the telecast from L.A. The Rams are playing the Vikings."

Michael was the man with whom I had been sharing my microwave oven, my salad spinner, and my body for nearly a year. When he moved in I expected to share something more with him than my bed and my appliances, but that, as it turned out, was a vain expectation. Physically, Michael was gorgeous; in bed he was pretty good, not as good as he thought he was, but still pretty good; around the apartment he was a total loss. And as for sharing any real concerns, that was not Michael's style. He would never be the sort of man you could wake up at three in the morning and confess that your dreams had been so haunted by the faces of starving babies in Angola that you'd just written a check on your joint household account for a thousand dollars and sent it to Oxfam.

The elevator bumped at our floor, and Michael raced through the apartment, flinging his jacket at the hall-tree—a failed pitch-out—and threw himself down on the living-room sofa as though he'd just come in third in the Boston Marathon. Panting, he switched on the television.

"Hey, they've started," he said, his tone aggrieved.

I stood at the window for a while, watching a melancholy November rain smudge the runners in Central Park. Then I left him to it, and treated myself to a long fragrant bath while I read another chapter in *Men Who Think They're Gods, and the Women Who Worship Them.* I tried to remember when we had last made love. It had been almost a week ago, right after Monday Night Football. Tonight, I was in the mood for a little

TLC again. I did a little tweezing. I did my hair. I dabbed *Frenzy* on my pulse-points, slipped into a peach-colored satin peignoir and insinuated myself onto the sofa beside Michael and turned off the sound.

"Darling," I said, my smile vivacious. "Listen. Listen. You can hear the rain plinking against the windows and the wind humming between the buildings. Autumn is here, my darling. The year is ending, and that always makes me sad. Let's go to bed. Let's make love and make love and make love until we don't know if we're alive or dead."

"Later, babe. It's only the third quarter. How about bringing me a beer?"

I brought him his beer. I poured it over his head. I poured it on his blue Pringle cashmere. I poured it down the crotch of his immaculately creased Ralph Lauren jeans.

"Are you crazy?" he yelled, jumping up. Together we watched the beer run down his pant legs and dribble into his Gucci loafers. "Have you got PMS or what?" He snatched the remote control from my hand.

"Not PMS—FMS—Football Mid-Season and I'm sick and tired of it. When we met you were this sweet sensitive guy who took me to plays and movies and gallery openings on Sunday afternoons. We even went to hear poets read. *Poets!* We talked from dusk to dawn. We never had enough time to say all the things we had to say to each other. We never had enough time in bed together. What happened? Was that the real you, or was it all just the courtship dance of the Manhattan Male? Michael? Michael! Turn off the sound and talk to me, Michael."

"Haven't you done enough?" He shook himself and looked down at the beer still frothing at his feet. "Liz, don't push me. I want to see this field goal." He fluttered a hand at me as though warding off a cloud of gnats.

I took an enormous deep breath, filling my lungs to the point of bursting. Slowly, very slowly I let it all out. Then I said, "Michael, would you, when the game is over, do something for me? Please."

He looked up grudgingly. "Now what?"

"Get out. Pack up your clothes, your lacrosse trophy, your Harvard-Yale game-ball and your self-cleaning garlic press, and get out of my life."

"Aw, Liz, have a heart! It's Sunday night."

I shrugged.

"For goodness' sake, Liz. Where'll I go?"

"You can sleep on that couch in your office. The one where you first made love to me." Michael sold stocks at Barrel, Pinch, Pilfer and Fudge. Looking back on it, I suspect all the brokers made out on that couch.

I left him staring at the screen and, heady with triumph, marched to the refrigerator where I pulled open the door of the top freezer and rummaged around—way in back of the ice cubes and the tortellini—until I found my secret cache of Häagen-Dazs Chocolate Chocolate-Chip. The carton had frozen to the shelf. I pulled. I swore. I yanked again. The ice cream cracked free, and I lurched backward clipping the Thanksgiving turkey with my elbow.

The turkey weighed eighteen pounds twelve ounces and it broke my foot in seven places.

My hospital room was fragrant with cut flowers. Get well cards, with offers of help appended, covered my nightstand, but it was Toni who brought me a yard-long Chinese back scratcher so that I could scratch my toes. It was Toni who fed me Chinese take-out so that I wouldn't starve to death on hospital muck. And it was Toni who brought me home from the hospital encumbered with crutches and a cast to the knee.

Toni took my keys and opened my apartment door for me. I took one look and screamed.

"Oh, my God! I've been robbed! Oh, my God! I've been robbed! Oh, my Go—"

"Stop that!" said Toni, tugging on my crutch. "You're getting hysterical."

"Why shouldn't I get hysterical? Look! Look! I've been robbed, for God's sake."

"Well, you said you told Michael to clear out. Maybe he, you know, got a little carried away."

"Michael may be a jerk, but he's not vindictive, and he's not a slob." The place looked as though Attila the Hun had played Genghis Khan on the Game of the Week. I pointed to a pile of rotting garbage on the coffee table. "Just look at that mess. Apple cores. Banana peel. Orange peel. Michael never eats fruit—it gives him hives. He couldn't have done it. Besides, he sent me a get well card from Maui."

"What's missing?" she said.

"*What's left?* would be more like it."

I crutched myself to a chair and sat glaring at the empty wall where my speakers had so proudly flanked my state-of-the-art stereo system.

"Count your blessings," said Toni. "At least they didn't take your records."

"Shut up!" I recommended.

"What's that?" said Toni. An official-looking enve-
lope was propped against a shriveled apple core. It was
stamped Special Delivery and Certified Mail. "They
must have signed for it. Your burglars must have signed
for it. Isn't that just too New York? Open it."

"I don't want to. Do you believe trouble comes in
threes?"

"I'll open it," said Toni.

"First I break my foot. Then I'm cleaned out. Whatever it says I don't want to know."

"Yes, you do," said Toni gently, looking up from the
letter. "Your building's going condo."

WHAT I TOLD BEN was an abbreviated version of the
facts. Even though I was sure he didn't imagine I had
been living with the Sisters of Chastity since I left college, I saw nothing to be gained by drawing pictures for
him. So I said, "First I was burgled, and then my building went condo. The burglars even signed for the certified letter that served as legal notice."

"That's New York," he said.

"I would have had to rob a bank to make the down
payment. Besides, I never really liked my apartment
that much anyway—it was really cramped—and Toni
had this great place she'd inherited from a director who
went to Hollywood to do just one picture. Everyone
knows what happens to off-Broadway directors who
say they're going to the Coast to do just one picture—
they never, ever come back. So I moved in with her."

After that we told each other horror stories about
apartment hunting. Every New Yorker has dozens of
them. Then Ben said, keeping his tone light, that he
sometimes wondered if his wife had married him be-

cause he had a bigger apartment than she did. He actually chuckled when he added that the marriage had lasted only until she met an interior decorator who owned a brownstone. That's when I knew I wasn't the only one tailoring the truth to fit the occasion.

It was very late when we walked the few blocks to my place. Walking beside him, I felt lithe and smooth. We paced along stride for stride, and it was almost as though my joints were oiled. Ben's sleeve kept brushing mine, sending tiny contact shocks up my arm.

At my door he turned to me with irresistibly wide eyes. "Would you like to go to a party tomorrow night? This friend of mine had a show of her sculpture last month, and she sold every piece. She's giving a party to celebrate, and I promised I'd go. You'll like her, I think. She's got this great loft."

That's when his eyes twinkled at me, and I felt as though I'd suddenly dropped two feet and come down hard.

"What time?" I croaked. For some reason my breathing seemed to have gone haywire.

"Nine o'clock?" He bent over me then, not as though he were preparing to kiss me, but more like he wanted to fix me in his memory until tomorrow. Very carefully, as though my hair were spun of spider's web, he tucked a lock behind my ear, and I turned my cheek into his palm. Just the merest touch.

"Nine o'clock, then," he said with a smile that would have melted bronze. And then he was gone.

TONI'S LIGHT WAS STILL on when I got home. I dumped my briefcase on my bed and went in to sit on the end of hers. She was sitting up in bed with a layout pad on her knees, doodling thumbnail sketches for a book jacket.

"So how was it?" she said. "Where did you go?"

"Bettina's. He lives just a couple of blocks away."

"That's handy." She applied herself to her pad for a moment. She sounded just the wee-est bit waspish, but I decided not to pursue it.

"I really like him, Toni."

"That's great." She tossed her layout pad to the floor and yawned. "I didn't realize it was so late. It's nearly two o'clock."

"He asked me to go to a party tomorrow night . . . tonight, actually."

She shrugged her French shrug. "That's great," she said, again, reaching for the light.

"I thought you liked him," I said.

"I do like him. I think he's just great." She turned out the light. "Good night, Liz."

I don't believe it, I told myself. *I absolutely refuse to believe it. If I didn't know Toni so well I'd think she was jealous.*

4

Ben

IF I HAD TEN BUCKS for every woman I've wanted to take out on a second date, I could retire to the West Indies and spend the rest of my life fishing for bonefish. And that being the case, I couldn't figure out why I was so nervous.

Liz sort of flowed into the taxi wearing a short black dress with little shimmery things all over it that winked when she breathed. The dress made her legs look as though they began somewhere up under her earlobes and went on forever, and she'd done something different with her hair. Last night it had been smooth and had swung in a blond curtain when she moved; now it was all wild strands and ringlets—like that Botticelli goddess of Spring. She should have had vines and flowers twined in her hair. I wanted so much to put them there that I had to shove my hands into my pockets so that she couldn't see them trembling.

Last night at dinner everything had been so easy, so smooth between us. Maybe it was the little shimmery things on her dress sparkling at me, or her hair all in ringlets, but I felt like I was sixteen again and going out on my first really big date with a shiny blue tie painstakingly knotted beneath my Adam's apple and a condom burning a hole in my wallet. I still remember filching that condom from my father's sock drawer. I was thirteen. By the time I was sixteen it had made a circular pattern on the outside of my wallet.

The taxi lurched forward throwing us both back against the seat, and Liz said, "You haven't told me whose party we're going to. I like to be prepared for these things, so you'd better tell me now. Is this someone whose work you really like, or do you put up with it because she's your friend?"

"Her name's Natasha Fleer. And yes, I do like her work. Usually."

"You don't mean the Natasha Fleer who shows at the Dace Gallery? Why, she's practically a legend. How could you not like her work? It's . . . it's . . ." She gestured futilely, defeated by her own enthusiasm.

I waited while she searched for the right word. When asked, Natasha would go so far as to describe her sculpture as forms on the verge of becoming. Evolving forms. Something like that, but her sculptures always conned me into believing that if I turned away and looked back suddenly I'd surprise an inscrutable tangle of shapes in the process of becoming something recognizable. But it never happened. Natasha created her originals in wax and had them cast in bronze by a foundry somewhere out on Long Island. Compared with most of the building-size sculpture you saw everywhere, her pieces were ridiculously small—about the size of a football. Because of all the hot beeswax she used, her loft-studio-apartment always smelled like a cathedral.

" . . . dynamic," Liz concluded lamely.

She laughed sheepishly and put a hand up to her hair in an elegant gesture that exposed the tender white inside of her wrist. I could smell her perfume—something light and ferny with a touch of lily of the valley and a hint of rain. I inhaled deeply. Any other woman I would have pinned to the seatback . . . but not Liz. Something held me back. Her natural elegance, perhaps, and the fact that I was having such a wonderful time just looking at her, just smelling her.

" . . . I'm never sure," she was saying, "what to say about art. I always feel so tongue-tied trying to talk about paintings and sculpture. But I suppose if paintings lent themselves to verbal descriptions, well, I suppose they'd be painted with words."

I don't know what I said at that moment, because my right thigh had started to twitch. I sat forward on the seat, clutching my kneecaps like a benched lineman, and willing myself to calm down.

"It's always the same," she continued. "Fleer may title her work *Ascending Forms*, or something like that, but I always see the same thing."

"Do you?" I finally managed.

"I've tried to see other things, I really have. But it's no good. I always see two people making love."

"So do I," I confessed. "But I've never admitted it to anyone before." She grinned and put her hand on mine and squeezed, and I would have been perfectly happy if the cab driver had kept driving south all the way down to the tip of Argentina.

I don't know of another feeling that matches walking into a party with the most desirable woman in the world on your arm. I walked into Natasha Fleer's party with Liz on my arm, and I felt like a million dollars. There never was a woman as beautiful as Liz that night.

Natasha's loft was jammed. There are lofts in New York and then there are lofts. Natasha's place was very sparsely furnished. In a space surrounded on three sides by floor-to-ceiling windows she had created what the architects call a designed environment. Little of this was visible, of course, because the loft was so crammed with people. It was like walking onto the floor of the New York Stock Exchange. There were artists, their friends, lovers, wives, and husbands. There were gallery owners and dealers. On our right, two museum directors stared into the cleavage of an *Art Age* critic as she held forth on Rothko. On our left, a sculptor who had built her career welding VW Beetle bumpers into direct metal sculpture bemoaned the dearth of raw materials. All around us artists' stocks rose and fell, futures were optioned, market forecasts buzzed everywhere, insider trading was what everyone hoped to get in on.

I grabbed a couple of drinks from a passing tray and found a window ledge where Liz and I could sit. The crowd ebbed and flowed around us.

"What do you think of it?" I said.

"The party?"

"Natasha's loft."

"I could never live up to it," she said.

I smiled my agreement, trying hard to keep my eyes on hers so that she wouldn't catch me staring down her cleavage. Her eyes were the greenest I have ever seen. Not yellow-green, or blue-green, but green-green. Like a newly mown infield under the lights. They seemed extra shiny looking up at me and extraordinarily large.

"The first thing I'd do," she said, "is put in walls. I like places cozy. This is too much like an airplane hangar. Yes, I'd put up lots of walls."

"I'd put in a fireplace," I said.

"Could you? I mean, is that allowed in a loft?"

"If it's done right. I'd install a big one with a stainless-steel flue."

"And bookshelves," she added. "You could put up miles of bookshelves in a place like this if you added some walls."

"Why not build freestanding shelves," I suggested. "They could be your walls instead of real walls."

She brushed her lower lip with a thoughtful finger. "It would certainly make for more light, wouldn't it..."

We talked on, remaking the loft, arguing over colors, furnishing it, as though we'd known each other for years. That's when Natasha appeared, fluting, "Ben, darling, there you are. I've been scouring the place looking for you." Natasha Fleer was almost as tall as I was. She had high Slavic cheekbones and vivid blue eyes and strong, square peasant hands. She wore a complicated green dress that reached the floor, and she'd fixed her dark hair in a difficult-looking knot from which three long oriental pins protruded.

I introduced Liz, and Natasha stepped aside to reveal a man who'd been lurking behind her.

"This..." said Natasha, with a milky smile that would have put Heidi to shame, "this is Raymond Raymond. He has a gallery on Prince Street. I promised to introduce you, darling. Raymond's writing a mystery novel. It's all about a gallery on Prince Street."

Raymond Raymond was short and chubby, his hand limp and his hips wide, and he snickered with nerves. He was all but perfect to audition for the Joel Cairo role in a remake of *The Maltese Falcon*, but something was missing.

Raymond Raymond looked up at me with hot eager eyes, and before I could protest, Natasha swept Liz away to meet a painter who was writing a novel about a painter. Liz smiled at me over her shoulder as she plunged into the crowd after Natasha, and I felt my insides lurch.

"So," Raymond began, as accusatory as a young DA on his first case. "You're Terence Ross's editor, aren't you?"

I nodded, pivoting to the right so that I could keep the beacon of Liz's golden hair in sight.

"I want only the best for my book," said Raymond.

"I'm sure you do," I said. "Now, if you'll excuse—" But I was too late. Four friends of Raymond's had joined us, encircling me as securely as a Roman cohort. Across the room I glimpsed a snapshot of Liz's wrist silhouetted against a blue flannel back.

"Let me tell you about my book," said Raymond, as though there were any way I could stop him short of garroting him with his own four-in-hand. "It opens four months before the actual murder takes place . . ."

I groaned inwardly and stared pensively at the shiny tops of Raymond's shoes. *Spats*, that's what was missing. In the movie, when Joel Cairo walked into Sam Spade's office he was wearing fawn-colored spats. Raymond droned on. I looked up at the sound of Liz's laugh bubbling into a sudden lull in the hubbub. She was way on the other side of the room, listening intently to a woman who appeared to be clad entirely in scarves. Nearby I saw Natasha absentmindedly ruffle her lover's hair. It was clear she had grown tired of him. George was a doe-eyed art critic who, at twenty-five, was not quite half Natasha's age. His body was so carefully developed that even his earlobes looked as though they'd been perfected by steroids.

"Younger lovers are all very well for the short term," Natasha had once told me. "They're so full of zip and vinegar—if you know what I mean. But I'm nearly sixty, and it's getting harder and harder to find something to talk about. George asked me the other day whether Adlai Stevenson was a Democrat or a Republican. Oh, Ben," she sighed. "Don't fall for a twenty-year-old bimbo. It's the death of civilized conversation."

Across the room I watched Clarise, Natasha's dealer, making glad-eyes at George. And a few moments later, I spotted Clarise's lover, John, doing the same thing.

"Look," I said to Raymond, taking him by the shoulders and spinning him around. "Do you see that man over there talking to George—Natasha's friend? He could do you a lot of good, Raymond. He's the biggest agent in Manhattan. Why don't you go over and introduce yourself, he's always looking for new talent. His name's Stevenson, Adlai Stevenson."

"He must be big," said Raymond. "I know I've heard the name before."

I jumped up on the windowsill and scanned the sea of bobbing heads until I spotted Liz and Natasha in the kitchen area doing something to trays of food. It took me ten minutes to work my way over to her, scoop her up, and get her away to myself.

"There's a staircase at the back of the pantry," I said. "Let's try for it." We wormed our way around a clutch of graphic designers debating the pros and cons of having a house style, and a woman, who must have been an architect, haranguing three men about some

new Manhattan building. Finally, we pressed on and up
the stairs, squirting out onto the empty roof like a pair
of champagne corks.

"This is wonderful," said Liz, twirling like a dancer
with her arms flung out and her head tilted back. Her
breath hung in the air in little silver puffs.

"It's cold up here," I said. "Let me get your coat."

"It's not cold, it's beautiful. Have you ever seen a
moon like that? It looks like part of a stage set. Let's sit
down." She led me to one of those twisted-limb garden
seats, and I put my jacket around her shoulders.

"How was your novelist?" I asked, not really caring.
All I wanted to do was look at her. She was right about
the moon. In its light everything was silvered—her hair
had turned platinum, her skin as white as porcelain.

"Dreary. How was yours?"

"He reminded me of Joel Cairo."

"You're right," she said, grinning. In the moonlight
her lips looked dark and moist. "All he needed was yellow chamois gloves and a lot of rings . . ."

"And a derby . . ." That's when I put my arm around
her and hugged her against me. It was so natural that
I'd done it before I even had a chance to think about it.
She didn't seem to mind. She even kicked off her shoes
and tucked her feet under her. I love it when women do
that, pointing one foot like a ballerina and pushing off
a pump with the toe of the other shoe.

She snuggled against me, my arm keeping her co-
cooned in my jacket. Then it began to snow—a flurry,
a swirl in the air of early spring snow. It was as if pieces
of the moon were swirling and eddying around us, the
moon shining on as brightly as ever. Snowflakes clung
to her hair like diamonds and melted on her cheeks like

dew. Tiny drops caught in her eyelashes, beaded her lips.

"Cybele," I said. "You are Cybele, Goddess of the Moon." Very slowly, very carefully, I licked the snow-flakes melting on her lips. Then I kissed her, and her lips were like sweet fruit, as soft as parting figs, moon-silvered figs, full and moist and yielding.

The snow fell, dissolving around us, and we kissed until we'd made ourselves so drunk with kisses we staggered against each other when we tried to stand. In the taxi back to Liz's place we held hands. And that was enough. Holding hands was enough.

5

IT WAS AFTER TWO when Ben left me at my door. I let myself in as quietly as I could so as not to wake Toni, and tiptoed down the hall to my room with my shoes in my hand—a bad actor's parody of stealth. A bar of yellow light shone out from under Toni's door. I could hear music playing. It was that American opera that starts with a lady reciting a menu to her butler. I can never remember the name of it. Or who wrote it. It's very sad—that I do remember—because the story turns on love denied.

"Hi!" I said to the door, tapping on it twice. "I'm home. Are you decent?" This was roommate's code for: Are you alone, or are you in bed with Ned?

The door opened, and there stood Toni in her David Hockney T-shirt, so long it brushed her calves. Her cheek was smudged with blue felt-marker; there was a yellow pencil tucked behind her right ear.

"Lizzie!" she whooped. "Who did your hair?" Her eyes were canny and amused. "It's marvelous! Turn around. I've never seen so many ringlets and tendrils. I love it. No wonder you weren't in your office when I called at five. You sly puss. I thought you were out having a drink with an author. How was the party?"

"Come talk to me while I get out of these clothes." We crossed the hall to my room, and I turned my back to her. "Do my zipper for me." I stepped out of my dress and, wincing, pulled off my earrings. "One of these days I'm really going to have to get my ears pierced. My earlobes are positively numb from these clip-ons. I think it's spreading. Even the back of my neck feels numb. Do you really like my hair like this?"

"I love it."

"Gigi talked me into it. Ben seemed to like it."

"It's terrific, I mean it." She stretched out on my bed, stuffed a couple of pillows behind her and locked her hands behind her head. "So how was it? Was there anyone there we know? Did you meet anyone interesting? How was Ben?"

I tossed my underthings on a chair and turned sideways to study myself in the full-length mirror. "Do you think my stomach looks poochy?"

"Poochy?" Toni groaned. "Give me a break. "I can count your ribs from here."

"I think I'll have my legs waxed."

Toni sat up, an appraising gleam in her eye. "You're falling in love, Liz. Yes, you are. I know all the telltale signs."

"Oh, don't be so silly. I hardly know the man."

"Only two dates and already you're talking about having your legs waxed? In my book, that's serious."

My answer was a nonchalant shrug. I wasn't entirely sure myself. I pulled on the burgundy velour tracksuit I'd found on sale at Bloomingdale's—"tracksuit" in this case is a style rather than a functional designation. The velour is silk and always makes me feel rich and cosseted, as though I am snuggling into a downy, silk cocoon. I flopped onto the bed beside Toni.

"Aren't you going to bed?" she said.

"I'm too revved up. I couldn't possibly sleep."

"Then tell me about the party. I want to hear everything. Absolutely everything. Take it from the top."

"The party, believe it or not, was at Natasha Fleer's—"

"The sculptor? How in the world does Ben know her?"

"I don't know. I gather they're old friends."

"Now that's odd. She just isn't someone your typical crime editor would know. Your Ben is getting curiouser and curiouser."

"He's not *my* Ben."

"What's she like?"

"I can't tell you much about her, we didn't have much time to get to know each other. We barely had time to talk—she was so busy working the room." I punched up the pillow behind my head. "Almost as soon as we arrived she saddled each of us with a pair of eager authors."

"Don't you just hate that? How was the food?"

"I'm afraid I don't really know."

Toni sat up and bent over me, her hands on my shoulders pinning me to the bed. "How can you say you don't know? You know you're not allowed to go to a party and come home without a report on the food. That's a house rule."

"I do have a report on the food—sort of."

Toni released me and sat back. "Go ahead."

"Miss Manners would have been proud of me. I ditched my author as quickly as good manners allowed, and headed for the kitchen area—"

"To eat?"

"No, silly, to try and find Ben. I couldn't see him anywhere, and I thought if I climbed up on a kitchen chair I might be able to spot him. I never had the chance. Natasha Fleer was twirling in place like a spinning green top, trying to unload all the hors d'oeuvres from six boxes at once. And the faster she twirled the more impassive all three waiters were. They were ready to pass trays of food, but not, apparently, prepared to lend the poor woman a hand."

"Union rules?"

"It didn't take me more than half a second to see that she was going to be up to her armpits in stuffed mushrooms if someone didn't pitch in, so I pitched."

"But where was the caterer?"

"Drunk. The caterer's man was drunk. He was sitting on the floor with his back propped against the fridge, keening. I could see what needed to be done, so I opened one box after another and kept shoveling out foie gras until all the boxes were empty. The waiters flowed in and out at their own stately pace, and the caterer's man finally threw his apron over his head, like Peggotty, and went to sleep on the floor. He was snoring like a steam train when Ben finally turned up. Natasha kissed both my cheeks, muttered something about being eternally grateful, and Ben took me away from all the hubbub and up on the roof."

"Who was on the roof?"

"No one. Not a soul. It was heavenly. Ben and I spent the rest of the evening up there talking. And that's why

I can't tell you anything about the food, other than what it looked like, because we never got around to eating any."

"And now I suppose you're hungry."

"Starved!"

"Pizza?"

"What else? With everything?"

"Everything."

In the kitchen Toni turned the oven on to preheat. We did not have a microwave oven. As much as she adored all gadgets—and anyone with French blood does, I've discovered—Toni did not believe in microwave ovens. Food is meant to be heated naturally. With heat. *Le Bon Dieu*, she said, did not give us the fruits of the earth so that we could bombard them with invisible beams. He may move in mysterious ways, she believed, but microwaving was not one of them. This from the woman whose most treasured possession is her compact disc player....

Toni opened a bottle of Côte du Rhône while I rummaged in the fridge for the bowl of black olives.

"How's Ned?" I asked, nibbling an olive and following it with a sip of wine. "Did he pick you up after work?"

Toni swirled the wine in her glass. Two vertical lines of concern appeared above her nose. She spoke without looking up. "His mind is someplace else these days. I know he's rushed off his feet with this part, but somehow when we're together...he's there, but he's not there."

"Toni," I said. "Look at me."

She looked up, and her eyes were pinched with hurt.

"Do you still love Ned? Because if you don't, maybe it's time to think about calling it quits?"

"I don't honestly know. Sometimes I think I love him. Love him passionately. And other times I think maybe he's just a habit. Maybe I'm too chicken to call it quits, or too cynical."

"You? Cynical? You're the most romantic person I know."

She shrugged her French shrug. "It's hard not to be cynical when your lover climbs into bed with a smile that has *audition* written all over it. But at least I know him, Liz. Ned's safe."

"Ned's safe? What is *safe* supposed to mean?"

"You know what I'm like if I don't have a man in my life. I get all twitchy and neurotic and end up feeling...you know, like a wild woman. Besides, these days what woman in her right mind would go to bed with a guy she doesn't really know? Ned and I have known each other for years, and I trust him. And he trusts me. He's safe."

"That's a lousy script," I said. "It's so bad it sounds as though you stole it from *Metropolitan Medical Center.* You've got to have a better reason than that for seeing Ned, and you know it. I think you're still more in love with him than you dare to admit. You pretend you're being all cool and analytical about your relationship, but when push comes to shove, you're still infatuated with him. You've been infatuated with him from the first moment you clapped eyes on his gorgeous profile, and that's why he's able to make your life so miserable. If he were just convenient and safe, he couldn't hurt you this way. If I still loved someone after an affair had started to go sour, I'd admit it."

Toni crossed her eyes at me and snorted.

"And you'd be the first to know," I insisted.

The timer pinged. It was an eight-function electronic timer; logical consistency was never Toni's longest suit.

Toni put the frozen pizza into the oven and leaned against the door, sipping wine. "I don't know. Maybe you're right, and I do still love him." She perched on the edge of the table and ate three olives, one after the other. Then she said, "I don't want to talk about Ned and me anymore. Tell me more about the party. What was Natasha's loft like?"

"The dominant motif was *flow*. The living areas flowed into the dining area that flowed into the kitchen area. I never did see the studio area, but something must have flowed into them. No walls anywhere, just flow, flow, flow." My hands swam through the air like fish. "It made me uneasy. All that unbroken space was unsettling. It would take all your energy just to live up to it, it was so perfect, so tasteful, so restrained. One look and of course I had this overwhelming urge to cover the whole place with English chintz."

Toni giggled. "Wouldn't you love to see a chintz loft? Wouldn't that be a hoot?"

"Paisley throws from Liberty..."

"Walls in dusty-plum..." Her eyes danced.

"Apricot and lime woodwork..."

"Peach chintz and aubergine for the curtains..."

"Ben and I did kid around about it. You know the way you do when you see a place that's full of possibilities. I said I'd put up bookcases, and he said he'd add a fireplace. That's a point in his favor, don't you think?"

"Wanting a fireplace?" She sipped her wine.

"I put it to you—as they say in all the best trial scenes—that a man who thinks in terms of fireplaces is a nester at heart."

"He might be a firebug." She glanced at me and then at the timer. It pinged, right on cue, and she busied herself sliding the pizza onto a platter, cutting it, and serving us each a piece. "What was all that you were telling me about going up on the roof with Ben? What did the two of you talk about up there?" She studied her pizza carefully, picked off a steaming slice of pepperoni, blew on it and chewed it, puffing in mouthfuls of cool air.

"Not much. Mostly we looked at the moon." I nibbled the cheesy point off my piece. "We sat together on one of those madly rustic garden seats—you know the kind I mean, all picturesquely gnarled twigs, and—"

"Forget the furniture. Cut to the action."

"There wasn't any action. Not in the usual sense. But what happened was . . . well, it was extraordinary. It really was. The moon—now you have to picture this— the moon was huge, enormous, with only the odd wisp of cloud here and there, and suddenly we were being snowed on."

"Snowed on? It couldn't have been snow. It must have been ash."

"No, really it was snow. It was all over in a minute or two. And the moon was shining the whole time. It was like being in an enchanted place. Ben put his jacket around my shoulders, and then he put his arm around me, and we just sat there together. I know it's hard to believe, but it was magical. And somehow just being together like that was enough."

"Didn't he even kiss you?"

"Not then. He didn't even try."

"What's wrong with him?"

"Nothing's wrong with him."

"Did he say anything? He must have said something. What did he say when this 'snow' started falling?"

"It *was* snow. And he said the most wonderful thing." I finished my pizza and slid another slice onto my plate.

"Tell, tell."

"It didn't melt. The snow. Not at first. And then it did. And it left his hair sprinkled with tiny diamond droplets—you've seen how black his hair is—well, I was thinking how absolutely gorgeous he looked at that moment, when he looked at me and his eyes were huge and shiny, like polished onyx, and he said . . ." I could feel my face flushing right up into my hair.

"But what did he say?"

"He said I was Cybele, Goddess of the Moon."

"He didn't!"

"He did, I swear."

"*Merveilleux!*"

"It was. I just sat there and sighed, hoping I didn't look like a cat thinking about a saucer of cream."

"It sounds like a movie. A French movie."

"Doesn't it? That's when he kissed me."

"Ah, at last. We come to the kiss. Was it a long kiss? A short kiss?"

"Middling."

"And on a scale of one to ten?"

I munched my pizza and grinned slyly. "I'd give it a twelve."

"You can't give it twelve. That's not fair. We set our scale at ten."

"That was before I'd been kissed by Ben Malloy. That man is really a kisser. Coming back in the taxi we didn't kiss at all. We held hands."

Toni sighed. "Do you suppose he has a brother?"

Ben

"HEY, BEN," Ross called. "Over here."

He was perched on a stool in my favorite coffee shop. I hated eating breakfast at home by myself. I liked to get out in the morning, get the feel of the city, feel it moving around me, coming to life. The Busy Bee over on Ninth Avenue was where I usually had breakfast during the week. Jimmy, the cook, knew how to fry eggs that weren't as tough as beer mats, and he served real Vermont maple syrup with his pancakes because his sister was married to a guy who worked for a syrup bottler up near St. Albans, so he got it at a good price.

I sat down and ordered eggs and bacon with toast and a side of hash browns. Cissie, Jimmy's wife, poured me a cup of coffee.

"That must have been some party last night," Ross said. "You have that glossy, smug look of a man who's been to one whale of a party."

"It was okay," I said. I sipped my coffee. Cissie made good coffee; it was so black and so strong it could bring a dying man to his feet and align him with true magnetic north.

"Did you take whatshername to the party? That editor you took to dinner?"

"Liz Crosby. Yes."

"So what happened?"

Cissie brought my breakfast. I chewed on a forkful of bacon and hash browns while I thought about what I wanted to tell Ross. There are some things you can talk about with your best friend and there are some things you can't. I swallowed and said, "We had a good time. Natasha's was crammed with the usual gaggle of arty types—you know what that scene is like—so I took Liz up on the roof for a while, and we talked. And then I took her home. The funny thing was…it snowed while we were up there."

"C'mon."

"There was this huge moon, looking as flashy and phony as a paper moon in a high school musical, and all of a sudden, out of nowhere…it started snowing."

"Snowing? It snowed last night? This is April. What is it, the twelfth? How could it snow?"

"Just that little bit. Just where we were…"

Ross pinched his lower lip with two fingers. "Been reading science fiction? Isaac Asimov send you a manuscript?"

"Don't give me a hard time, Ross. I don't know about where you were, but where we were, just for a minute or two, it snowed." I mopped up a last bit of egg yolk with a crust of toast and finished my coffee.

"So what happened when you took her home? Did you make out?"

"She's not that kind of woman."

"What do you mean, she's not that kind of woman? What other kind is there? If someone has added another sex, I'm sure I would have read about it in the *Times*."

"Shut up, Ross."

I wasn't going to tell him how I lay awake for hours after I took Liz home. I hadn't wanted to sleep. I wanted to remember. Remember the snow-diamonds glistening in her hair, remember the sweet softness of her parting lips. I knew it was corny, but I felt like a kid reviewing his first big date. I couldn't let the memory go. I reran every move over and over again. The moon, the snow, the sweetness of her mouth, her breasts pressing against me. The moon, the snow, the sweetness...

Just thinking about her made me feel young and foolish and giddy; remembering her I felt strong. Potent. One thing I was sure of after I'd played the scene in my head a thousand times: I wanted Liz. Wanted her totally. I ached to take her inside me, to keep her deep inside, against my heart. I know it sounds crazy. It is crazy. But that's what I wanted. If I could have swallowed her whole, I would have. The scary part was that I knew that if I ever did manage it, I'd never be able to let her go. And not being able to let go of a woman was my idea of terror.

Ross broke into my reverie. "You want to go to the gym after work? You look like you could use a good workout and a steam. Meet me at the gym at six-thirty? What do you say, Tiger?"

"Sure," I said, feeling as weak as a kitten.

6

Liz

"LIZ, DARLING," breathed the smoky-topaz voice of Gillian Ypes. "We must talk."

"Mumf," was the best I could manage before clapping my hand over the phone and yawning like a walrus. Toni and I had talked the small hours away, talked until the sun fought through the morning haze to lay an accusing yellow finger on the kitchen clock. There seemed little point in going to bed at twenty past seven, so we showered, drank the best part of a whopping pot of coffee and went in to the office. Now, it was nearly one o'clock, and I was definitely beginning to fray around the edges. I'd drunk enough coffee to replace all my red blood cells with caffeine molecules, but I was still ready to sell my soul for a ninety-minute nap. We used to do this all the time when we were in our twenties. We never had time for sleep. I don't know how we did it.

But now I had to deal with Gillian, an ex-Broadway actress who brought her first book to me because I had once spent a week in London with her theatrical agent-nephew.

"I'm sorry, Gillian," I said into the phone. "I didn't quite make it to bed last night. I'm afraid I'm just a bit muzzy today. You must be wondering when you can expect to see your contract for *The Ladies at Sunset*."

"Forget the contract. I'm withdrawing the book proposal."

"But why?" I couldn't very well tell her I'd spent an eternity talking Mr. Pomfret around to it. "It's going to be a splendid book."

"No, it's not. It's never going to be a book at all."

"Gillian, I don't understand what you're talking about."

"Richard stole my manuscript."

"That's preposterous," I sputtered. Gillian and Richard had been living together for almost thirty years— since they'd first played together in summer stock. "Are you absolutely sure he took it? I mean you know what your desk is like. Did you look in—"

"He took it. I wanted you to be the first to know. As soon as I hang up I'm calling the police, and then I'm calling the newspapers."

"Oh, no! Wait a minute," I said. "You don't want to do anything rash. Remember our Mr. Pomfret. Think of your career. You've met Hadley Pomfret. He's from an old, old New York family, with old, old, money. He does not like fuss. He does not like notoriety. Mr. Pomfret despises authors with messy private lives that get splashed all over the press. He's the last of his kind."

"To hell with your Mr. Pomfret. I'm calling the cops. I'm calling the gossip columnists. I'm calling all the TV networks. When I get my hands on that little toad I'm going to string him up by his—"

"Gillian, Gillian, please. Tell me exactly what happened. Take it from the top."

"Richard's having an affair. And don't tell me you don't believe it, because it's true. I asked him, and he denied it. It was the guiltiest reading I've ever heard. It reeked of subtext! We had a flaming row. I threw his Baccarat whisky decanter at him. It smashed into a million pieces, I'm happy to say. Then I locked myself in the bathroom and wept like a faucet. When I came out, he was gone. It wasn't until this morning that I discovered the little rat had filched my manuscript."

Lovers' quarrels, I thought. Deliver me from writers in the throes of lovers' quarrels. I did my best to sound good-natured and soothing. "Surely the script is the least of your worries. You can print out another copy of your manuscript, but you can't print out a copy of Richard."

"I wouldn't take Richard back if he came on a Tiffany platter with a diamond in his navel. And no, I can't print out the script. The weasel snatched my floppy disks."

That's when I nearly dropped the phone. "Can you reconstruct it? Couldn't you just go on from those first chapters I showed to Mr. Pomfret? They're right here on my desk somewhere."

"It's impossible. He has my notes—everything was on disk. I promise you, Liz, when I get my hands on that man I'm going to kill him."

I still couldn't believe it was as serious as she did. "Richard's bound to return," I said, trying to sound like the voice of reason. "And when he comes back he'll bring everything with him. I don't understand why he took it. He's always loved your books."

"Not this one. He's in it. The whole middle section is about us."

Now that put a different light on things. "Where is he?"

"If I knew, he'd be dead, I swear to you. I just wanted you to know before I call the police. Who knows, they may want to talk to you. I hope you'll cooperate."

"No, wait," I said. "Don't call anyone."

"I want my book back."

"Of course you do. And so do I, that goes without saying. But the police are busy, Gillian. Very busy. Let's be realistic here. The police are not going to fall all over themselves looking for Richard and your floppy disks, not when they're so busy with murder, rape, arson, drug busts, muggings, prostitution—you'll be lucky if they don't hang up on you."

"But I'm a taxpayer," she wailed indignantly.

"Aren't we all? That and fifty cents will get you a gumball."

"Then what do you suggest?"

"I know a man who knows everything there is to know about detecting," I said.

"But can he find Richard?"

"Of course he can. Trust me, Gillian. You'll have your book back before you know it."

"We'll see," she said, her voice bristling with skepticism. "I'll give him a week. If I don't have my book back in seven days, I'm going to the police and the press. Maybe I'll even go to Mike Wallace."

"Don't worry," I said, trying to sound optimistic. "My friend will find your book."

"I see him sometimes, you know. At Patsy's."

"Richard?"

"Mike Wallace. The last time he had linguine . . ."

"You're not going to tell Mike Wallace. Gillian, please, promise me."

"All right," she said doubtfully, "but I do have one stipulation. When your man finds Richard and recovers my book for me, I want him to break the bastard's kneecaps."

Hell hath no fury... I thought as I hung up. I couldn't tell which made her angrier, Richard having an affair or the loss of her book.

Even under the most ordinary circumstances, writers need constant reassurance. Something is always causing them the most infernal pain—usually it's their work. If you add to that the stinging slings and quiverful of arrows of the emotional life of any normal adult, and then factor in the sensibilities of an ex-actress who writes, like Gillian, you have a writer who is always on the edge of emotional chaos. Of course she had a right to be hysterical—what Richard had done was absolutely unforgivable. If I found him before she did, I'd maim the swine myself.

I walked out of my office carrying a pile of jacket proofs and a manuscript. These were props, weapons in my duel with Gudrun who was determined to prove me feckless. I never left my office empty-handed.

Gudrun looked troubled. Furrows of concern creased her Olympian brow. "Have you seen Buzz Bailey's corrected galleys?" she said. Buzz was one of our bestselling authors.

"Not yet. I've been waiting for him to send them back."

"They are back. They came in yesterday, and I haven't seen them since."

"Don't worry," I counseled for the second time that morning. "They'll turn up—just like the manuscript that went missing. I mean, we may misplace things around here, but we never really lose anything."

I tried to affect an air of confidence, but it was all show. We might have been relaxed in our procedures at the Press, but we were never careless or slipshod. And when I thought about it, I couldn't remember that we had ever, not even once, lost anything. An author's set of corrected galleys could not possibly evaporate into thin air. Where were they? It was worrying.

I stopped at Ben's office. The door was ajar, so I knocked. I pushed the door open a bit more and walked in. The office was empty, but after a moment or two the hair on the back of my neck began to prickle, and I had the distinctly uneasy feeling that eyes were boring into my back. I whirled around—no one. And then, on the top of the bookshelf nearest the door, I saw it: a black, foot-high statue of a malevolent bird. I was trying, unsuccessfully, to stare it down when Ben walked in carrying a cup of coffee.

"Good morning," he said, his eyes dancing so that I had to press my bundle of papers against my chest to keep them from rattling. He walked right up to me and stopped about six inches away. Neither of us moved to sit down. We just stood there staring at each other, and getting so high on what we saw we might have been drinking champagne.

"Hi," I finally managed. Me, Miss Mouth, Liz the Lip, star of my high school debate team, and the best I could muster was a monosyllable!

"You've met my bird," he said. "A gift from a writer who knows I'm a Hammett fan. It's corny, I know, but

I can't shove it in the back of a closet without hurting its feelings."

"Ben, I had a wonderful time last . . ."

"So did I," he said slowly.

"I have to talk to you, Ben. I want to ask you a favor."

"Anything," he said with a smile that turned my kneecaps to pudding. "Would you like some coffee?"

"No, thanks, I'm awash with it." I yawned hugely. "I didn't really sleep last night," I admitted.

"Neither did I."

We sat on the old leather sofa, I with my pile of manuscripts on my lap, Ben with his coffee mug balanced on his knee.

Ben said, "I told Ross about our miniature snowfall last night. He didn't believe me."

"Toni didn't believe me, either," I said. "Maybe it wasn't real. Maybe we imagined it."

"A folie à deux?"

"If you like," I said.

"I like it very much," he said, his black eyes huge and glittering and soft all at the same time.

"Well," I began, peeling my tongue from the roof of my mouth. My mouth had suddenly gone dry. "I have this little problem I was hoping you might be able to help me with."

"Anything," he said. "Anything at all."

I dropped my voice, in case Gudrun's ear might be flattened against the keyhole. "This is absolutely confidential. Top secret. Or dire consequences will ensue. And I mean dire."

Ben suddenly remembered the mug in his hand. He set it on the floor between us and moved closer. "What's wrong?" he whispered, the perfect accomplice.

First I told him about the manuscripts and galleys disappearing. He listened with grave interest. "Have you missed anything?"

"No," he said thoughtfully, "but I agree with you there's something sinister about all this."

"There's more." As succinctly as I could, I told him all about Gillian and Richard. I explained to him Mr. Pomfret's views on notorious writers. I even sketched for him how hard I had worked to talk Mr. Pomfret into buying the now stolen book—that now, Mr. Pomfret, who had always been somewhat suspicious of Gillian Ypes, was going to have his worst fears confirmed. As was I, for if Pomfret decided I was a fool, Gudrun the Goth would grind me to dust beneath her chariot wheels.

"The one thing we think we know for sure is who took Gillian's book, so at least that can't be related to what's been going on here. Can it?"

"I really don't think so, but I'm worried sick. I told Gillian you knew all about detecting..."

"I don't know anything about detecting..."

"She said if you don't find her book in a week..."

"I wrote my senior thesis on Dashiell Hammett's detective *novels*."

"...she's going to the poli— What do you mean you don't know anything about detecting?"

"I *edit* detective fiction. You know how little fiction has to do with the real world."

"Fiction," I said, in my most withering tone, "has everything to do with the real world." I looked up at his

Maltese falcon, perched as portentously as Poe's raven, above his chamber door. "Right," I said, standing up. "If you won't help me, I'll find the book myself."

THIRTY MINUTES LATER Ben and I walked into Frank Ypes's office. He was Gillian's nephew and Richard's agent. This seemed the most logical place to start looking. No actor is ever more than a phone call away from his agent.

Frank Ypes's secretary looked like what she surely was—a soap opera supporting actress down on her luck. I gave her my name, and she recited two carefully rehearsed paragraphs on the reasons Mr. Ypes couldn't see me. I told her to take in my card anyway. Thirty seconds later Frank came out of his office with his arms wide and the same fond, lopsided, Huck Finn grin that used to seem so sweet.

"Liz, darling," he burbled heartily. "Come in, come in."

I introduced Ben who stared hard at Frank and then at me. The three of us sat down. There was enough tension in the air to light the World Trade Center.

"Frank," I said. "Where's Richard?"

"I was afraid you'd ask me that," said Frank.

"What are you afraid of?" said Ben. I don't know how he did it, but his tone was menacing. Something in the way he said it suggested Frank would do well to be afraid of him.

Frank swallowed hard, and I watched the color drain from his face. "I can't tell you, Liz," he said, but he kept his eyes on Ben. "I'd like to, but I can't. I promised Richard."

Ben stood up, walked over to Frank's desk and sat on the corner nearest him, towering over him. Frank half rose from his chair, but Ben put his hand on his shoulder and pushed him back down. "No one is interested in your client's personal life, Frank. You don't mind if I call you Frank, do you, Frank? If your client fell in the East River, your Aunt Gillian would do a fan dance in Times Square at high noon. But your client stole something that belongs to Miss Ypes. Your client is a felon, Frank. And Miss Ypes is so eager to call the cops and the newspapers, that she's given us only twelve hours to get her property back from your felonious client. You're an accessory after the fact, Frank. You're indictable. Have you ever spent a night on Rikers Island, Frank?"

Sweat ran in rivulets down Frank's pasty face. He opened his mouth to speak, but nothing came out. I could see his shirt plastered to his chest.

Ben leaned over Frank, grabbed a large handful of shirtfront and jacket and lifted him right out of his chair.

Frank squeaked. Ben dropped him back into his chair. Frank pulled out his handkerchief and wiped his face. "I don't know where Richard is. Really, I don't. I haven't seen him. I don't know what he might have stolen from Gillian, but I don't want any part of it. Richard's been like an uncle to me for most of my life, but Liz, you know what their relationship is like—someone's always stomping off in highest dudgeon with threats of vengeance. A quiet Sunday with the two of them is like a Shakespearean matinee done by a bad rep company. I don't want to be caught in the middle of this. If you want my opinion, this whole thing is crazy.

Richard left a shopping bag with my secretary this morning before I got in. His instructions were for me to put it in my safe."

"Where is it?" I said. "That's Gillian's property."

"It's right here." He swung open the door of an old-fashioned green safe and handed Ben a Bloomingdale's shopping bag.

All three of us looked in the bag. A box of floppy disks lay on top of a stack of manuscript pages and file folders.

"That's it, isn't it?" said Frank. "That's Gillian's book." To his credit he looked ashamed of what his client had done.

"Frank," I said. "Is Richard having an affair? Gillian's convinced he is."

"I don't know. And if you find out, don't tell me. I don't want to know."

"BEN, YOU WERE WONDERFUL." I tried not to gush. It was hard. I'd been admiring his profile as we sat in a grid-locked taxi on the way to Gillian's, the shopping bag on the seat between us. For the first time I thought I understood the attraction of the hard-boiled detective novel. Here was this urbane man who, in the blink of an eye, could transform himself into Sam Spade, detective. How many other personalities did Ben have waiting for me to discover?

"Really, you were terrific."

"All in a day's work, ma'am," he said with a self-deprecating grin. "Always happy to be of service."

"I'm very grateful. I'm not at all sure Frank would have given this stuff to me."

Ben looked me up and down, slowly, before he spoke. "Hmm, I think he might. You shouldn't underestimate your... persuasiveness."

"There's nothing to be snide about. Frank and I were a thousand years ago. And it only lasted for a week. In another country..."

"Why are you telling me this?"

"I don't honestly know. I...I want to be honest with you, Ben. I want to be myself. No masks, no deceptions, just me."

That's when he kissed me, over the top of the shopping bag. "No masks," he said. "No deceptions."

We finally got to Gillian's apartment, but she'd gone out. After a brief consultation we took the shopping bag back to the Press with us. It was far too valuable to leave it with Gillian's concierge. I felt so good about what we'd accomplished—and of course about Ben's kisses, and our no deceptions pact—that I returned to the Press in a decidedly benign mood. I startled Mr. Pomfret with my cheery, "Hi!" when I passed him in the hall. I chirped at poor sad Mr. Grice as he scurried into the elevator. I even smiled at Gudrun who was ostentatiously laying a packet of proofs on my desk.

"Wonderful day," I said to her. Not having heard me come through the door, she jumped a foot.

I dialed Gillian's number and left a message on her answering machine. "I've got everything you're missing," I said. "We didn't want to leave it with anyone but you, so we brought it to my office. Stop worrying. I'll deliver it myself tomorrow, or I'll send it over by bonded messenger."

I could see Gudrun's antennae waving frantically for any incriminating morsel she might pick up. There was no way I was going to tell her about Gillian's missing manuscript, or Ben's and my little caper.

"Gudrun, what with one thing and another, I completely forgot to eat lunch. Call the deli, and tell them to send over two roast beef sandwiches, rare and with all the trimmings."

Gudrun, for whom the Four Last Things were carrot juice, wheat germ, brown rice and tofu, glowered at me as though I'd ordered fricassee of Easter Bunny. When she went off to place my order, I invited Ben to share my lunch.

My euphoria lasted until Gillian returned my call the next morning.

"You've got everything back?" said Gillian. "How marvelous. Where did you discover the thieving Richard? No, don't tell me. I don't want to know. I'm wiping every trace, every vestige of him out of my life forever. Are you going to bring my manuscript over yourself, or send it? I'd rather you brought it. After what I've been through, I can't bear the thought of some stranger carrying it around. He might be mugged."

"Don't worry," I said in my most soothing tone. "I'll deliver it to you with my own two hands." I swung round in my chair as I talked and pulled open my file. "It's right here in my file." But it wasn't there.

7

Liz

"Liz? Are you still there?"

"Gillian...darling..." I took a deep, deep breath before I trusted myself to speak again. "My day is absolutely crammed. You know how it is—of course you do—but I promise you'll have your manuscript in your hands by seven o'clock tonight."

I hung up and whipped out the door pausing only long enough to instruct Gudrun. "If Gillian Ypes calls, I'm in a meeting."

Ben's office was empty. "He's with Mr. Pomfret," said a disembodied voice. Paul strode toward me chewing on his thoughts. A fellow fiction editor, Paul does his best thinking while pacing. In his baggy old blue blazer and ancient brogues, he haunts the halls of the Press like the Ghost of Publishing Past—in comparison to Mr. Grice who, with his computer printouts and holy bottom line, is the Ghost of Publishing Yet To Come.

"Anything the matter, my dear? You look a bit whitish."

"Really? Me? Pale. It must be my new lipstick."

"I had a very troubling call this morning," said Paul. "One of my writers said he'd received a letter from my secretary requesting an additional copy of his most recent revisions on chapters ten and fifteen. She wanted these because she couldn't find them in the revised manuscript he sent back to us. She simply assumed he'd forgotten to include them. But he swears he did include those chapters. He states further that two of his friends, whom we also publish, have received similar letters."

The ugly troll of dread that had been lurking in the back of my mind grew larger.

"This makes the Press look very bad," Paul continued. "It does nothing to instill confidence in our authors. Mine had some very harsh things to say. If this continues, he'll move to another house . . ." Paul stared sadly at his toe caps.

"It's been happening to me, too." I said. "I thought I was the only one. First a manuscript disappeared and then turned up with three chapters missing. Then a set of author-corrected galleys. Now a book in rough draft. Why, Paul? While it's all terribly embarrassing, everything that's been taken could be replaced without an enormous amount of fuss. Except, of course, the draft that I discovered missing this morning. I simply do not understand it. There's always another copy of a manuscript or a galley someplace. So why this nastiness? What's the point of it?"

"Perhaps embarrassment *is* the point, you see. Doubt, insecurity, they'll drive our authors out the door like lemmings. Like lemmings, yes . . ." and he paced away, following his toe caps down the hall, while I stood rooted to the floor trying to figure out who would want to drive our authors away.

On the way back to my office I walked smack into Gudrun coming out of the ladies' room.

"Look," she said, holding the Bloomingdale's shopping bag aloft as though it were a trophy of war. "I just found this in the john. It was jammed under the couch. Isn't this the bag I saw you put in your file yesterday? Here, look inside. The pages are all slugged 'Ypes.'"

"Gudrun, you've saved my life. I owe you one."

The odd thing was that after Gillian's book turned up, things at the Press were absolutely quiet. For a while we all waited for yet another shoe to drop, but when nothing more followed, people stopped holding whispered conferences around the watercooler, and in the end we put it down to a run of flukes and particularly rotten luck.

However, the afternoon Ben and I had joined forces to winkle out Gillian's bits and pieces from her nephew Frank cemented something between us. Almost every day after that Ben would wander into my office, coffee cup in hand, and I'd put aside the manuscript I was working on, and we'd talk. Sometimes we'd have dinner together, after which he always kissed me goodnight at my door, but nothing more. If I asked him in, he declined. I couldn't figure it out. Toni and I discussed it endlessly.

"What do you think he's waiting for?" said Toni. "A sign in the sky, or something?"

"I can tell from the way he kisses me that he's holding himself back. I can feel the tension in him. As though he's holding himself in by some tremendous effort of will."

"The big question is why?"

"He has to know how much I want him. He ought to be able to feel that. He must be able to feel that. In a way he's behaving like those Olympic athletes you see pacing around like so many coiled springs, psyching themselves up for the pole vault."

It was about a week later that Ben popped into my office around six and asked me to dinner. The surprising thing was that when I told him I couldn't go because I had to finish a line-edit on a manuscript, he wasn't nearly as disappointed as I expected him to be. He didn't plead with me to change my mind, he just said, "Right!" and walked out of my office. I think I was a bit miffed at that.

It must have been nearly nine o'clock when he strode into my office and literally pulled me out of my chair. "Not finished yet? Time for a break. Come to my office." His black eyes danced with excitement as he led me along the empty corridor. The Press was deserted.

"Ben, what are you up to? I can tell from the look on your face, you're up to something. Ben? I've got so much to do. This is no time for pranks. I'm never going to get caught up if—"

That's when I saw it. The battered coffee table in front of his old leather sofa was laid with white linen. Candles blazed in a pair of silver candle holders. There was champagne in a bucket of ice and crystal flutes from which to drink it. Two places were set with black plates and a first course of roasted red peppers and Roquefort, one of my favorites. There was a black platter of boned stuffed chicken in jelly, and a bowl of potato salad. Surely the most elegant picnic these ancient offices had ever seen.

"Ben this is absolutely marvelous. You've been conspiring with Bettina, you sly puss." There isn't another chef in New York who can touch the hem of her apron when it comes to boned chicken stuffed with pistachio nuts.

"Hungry?" he asked, grinning from ear to ear.

"Starved!" The way he looked at me when I said "starved" was something new. There was confirmation in his look and agreement about something that had nothing to do with food. I knew from the way his eyes dived into mine when he so carefully placed the champagne flute between my fingers that he had made a decision. I could only wonder, *Why now?* We raised our glasses to one another, our eyes locked over the rims in a silent toast, and we both knew exactly what was going to happen.

We ate slowly, deliberately, and silently. Perhaps it was this silence that made it so peculiarly, so uniquely exciting. Two people whose lives are words uttered none. We had thrown them off. We didn't need them. In our journey to this point we had traveled beyond them. We used our senses instead, watched and listened, listened to inner voices. Ben studied my hands as I ate as though he'd never seen such clever things before. I gazed with untiring delight at his muscles working in his jaw as he chewed. When he licked his lips, my breathing simply stopped. I could hear my heart tomtoming against my ribs. I heard the sofa creak when he leaned forward to pour more champagne. The fizzing bubbles sounded like distant sparklers on the Fourth of July.

Ben opened another bottle of wine, filled our glasses and stood up. He left me sitting on the sofa and crossed the room to perch on the edge of his desk. He leaned back, his feet wide apart, his hands poked into his pockets. He made it very plain that whatever it was he wanted to say, he needed distance to say it. His voice, when he finally spoke, was so soft I had to lean toward him, straining to catch every word.

"That night we went to Natasha's party. . . when we sat together on the roof in the moonlight . . . and it snowed and it was like pieces of the moon dusting your hair...that's when I started falling in love with you..."

"Oh, Ben," I whispered. "I know."

"I want to make love."

"Yes."

"Liz, are you sure . . . about this?"

"Yes." I stood up, but I didn't move any closer.

"I want to tell you what I think love is. I think it's like a train journey in a dream—once you get on, you can't get off. It's a runaway train cannonballing down the track at a hundred miles an hour. It won't stop and you don't know where it's going. It could kill you or . . ."

"Or what?" I said, walking slowly toward him, not stopping until I stood close to him, in the V of his thighs.

"Or it could take you to a place you have never dreamed existed."

"Take me there, Ben."

"I don't ever want to hurt you, Liz."

"You won't hurt me, Ben."

"I've got to tell you now, I don't want you to have any illusions. I'm not the marrying kind. Once was enough."

"I don't have any illusions, Ben. I only know I want to get on that train with you." How could I say no when I wanted him more than anything in the world? I had promised myself after the debacle with Michael that I would never again get involved with a man when I could clearly see it would be a no-win relationship. And if ever there was a zero-sum relationship it would be Ben and me. Of course it was absolutely irrational even to contemplate such a thing. But I wanted him, wanted him every bit as much as I knew he wanted me.

"We don't know where this train's headed. It might be a rough ride."

Perched as he was on the edge of the desk, our heads were on the same level, and I pressed my palms against his chest, sliding my hands beneath his jacket. I stepped closer until I could feel his body, lean and hard against mine. "I'm going with you," I said.

He kissed me then. Kissed me as he had never kissed me before. It began slowly and languorously, probing and tender, the way we had kissed on the roof, but now there was a hungry urgency as his mouth devoured mine, lighting fires deep inside me, starting flutters of raw desire. His arms closed around me, and his hands, with tantalizing slowness, with sweet explorations, began their slow descent until they closed over my bum. The fires within me were raging now, and he drank from my mouth as though to quench a thirst born of a lifetime of desire. When he touched my breast I thought I would explode right there, I wanted him so much. I pressed my hips against his until I could feel the urgent hardness of him, the heat of him. Slowly, very, very slowly, I began moving my hips. Ben groaned then, his mouth still pressed against mine.

We stumbled—a single, four-legged clinging creature—over to the sofa. We had trapped ourselves in a delicious lovers' dilemma. We wanted so desperately to be out of our clothes, but we couldn't let go. We settled it finally, by lying side by side and opening each other's buttons. It was like opening a present. In the flickering candlelight his skin was a deep gold, his chest muscles sharply defined beneath a butterfly of curly black hair. Short black fuzz arrowed down his hard belly. His skin smelled as sweet as apples.

By some sleight of hand, my bra disappeared and was replaced by his eager hands. He cupped my breasts, cradled them and kissed them, nuzzled them, all with such delight he made me believe he had never seen a breast before in his life, although he knew exactly what to do with one. He was so wonderful I laughed in my pleasure—something I had never done before in my life. There was such joy in Ben's lovemaking, such giving in his caresses. His fingers, his hands, his mouth, his tongue, every touch brought a new delight. I was flushed with desire, aflame for him.

I wrapped my arms around his back. It was my turn to slide my exploring hands down his rippling back, my turn to grip his hard buns in my urging hands, my turn to groan with an infinity of pleasure as I guided him into me, astonished at the heat and the hardness of him, the perfect rightness of him. For a moment we just fitted together, unmoving, smiling at each other in perfect understanding. Then Ben began to move, slowly, oh, so deliciously slowly. Then quicker and quicker and quicker. I closed around him as he thrust into me, deeper and deeper, my legs locking him to me. He groaned rhythmically as he moved, straining, throbbing—a volcano erupting within me, hot lava bubbling through my veins. I felt him pushing my deepest places into wild spasms of aching joy.

"Oh!" I cried. "Oh!" as the spasms increased. This was so far beyond anything I had ever felt before, I thought I would burst. "I don't think I can stand it." I was gasping for breath.

"Do you want me to stop?"

"No!" I shouted, my hips arching to meet his powerful thrust. "Please don't stop. Oh, please don't ever stop."

Somehow, he found his way even deeper into me, and we came together in an explosion like a blinding light. I think I passed out.

When consciousness returned I found myself cradling Ben in my arms, his head heavy and oh, so sweet on my breast. It was as though we had feasted on each other, gorged ourselves till our skins were tight and sleek. We lay very still, while the sweat dried on our bodies, and the old leather sofa creaked as we breathed. The candles guttered.

"Oh, Liiiiizzzz," Ben said, drawing the sound out, lingering over it, his voice soft, muzzy, caressing.

WHEN AT LAST Ben brought me home, I didn't ask him in. I wanted to be alone then, and Ben seemed to understand this without my saying a word; that was one of the thousand astonishing things about this astonishing man—his ability to know what I was thinking. I'd never known a man who could tune in to me the way Ben did. I suppose it's a sexist thing to say, but intuition is such a rare thing to find in a man. I wanted to be alone, because I wanted to curl up in my own bed and think about what had happened. I wanted to remember everything, savor everything all over again. What I had experienced with Ben was so amazing it was going to take a little getting used to. Was there ever such a lover as Ben? Let's not kid ourselves, there are your common, or garden-variety orgasms, the *well-that-was-nice-would-you-like-a-cigarette?* sorts of orgasms; and then there is the other kind, Ben's kind—all wildly contracting muscles I didn't even suspect I had, until I went quite wild in his arms, a ravening Amazon.

The experience of being loved by a man like Ben has got to alter a woman's view of herself, her life, her view of her place in our spinning universe. I suppose I should have been wary, but I was exultant. I had never felt so much a woman in my life. I yawned and stretched on my cool sheets; I could feel myself drifting off. I pressed my palms against my cheeks, and I could smell Ben on my fingers—a pungent mix of spice, and forest fern, and his sweat mingled with mine. I touched my throat still taut from his kisses, my breasts aching now for his hungry mouth. I stroked my silky skin thinking, here he did this, here he did that, until I felt my body grow heavy with remembered love.

I was lost, and I knew it. I didn't know where Ben might lead me, but I knew wherever he went I would follow.

I WAS SITTING at the kitchen table the next morning, smiling into my coffee cup, when Toni shuffled in wearing her Capuchin-brown robe and flip-flops. Her eyes were half-closed, and she groped her way to the coffeepot. She looked like a crabby monk.

"I never even heard you come in last night. What did you do, spend the night at the office doing line-edits? You must be dead on your feet." She studied me with an appraising eye as she sipped her coffee. "You don't look dead on your feet. You look . . ." She thought for a bit, and then she said, "You look sleek and glossy. And smug. You look like a woman with a delicious secret . . ." She drank some more coffee. "In fact, you look like a woman with a hickey on her neck who has been well and truly laid."

I smiled what I hoped would look like a Mona Lisa smile, and spread plum conserve on a piece of buttered toast.

"You didn't!"

I nodded.

"Well, hallelujah! At last. I was beginning to give up hope. But where? I was here all night. His place?"

"His office."

"No!"

"On the sofa."

"Well, tell me. Tell me everything." She leaned toward me, her elbows on the table, her cup cradled in her hands.

And I did tell her everything. Well, almost everything. And when I'd finished she said, "Okay now, considering that on a scale of one to ten we have agreed to rank my Ned at 7.8 and your late Michael at 8.1, where would you rank Ben?"

"We have to revise our scale. Ben is right off the charts—somewhere around fifteen."

"C'mon!" she snorted, shaking her head in disbelief.

"It's true. I swear it. I've never had orgasms like that in my life before."

"*Orgasms*—plural?" Her voice rose to a squeak. "How many did you have?"

"I lost count."

"I don't know how you do it. I really don't. What have you got that I don't have?"

"It's just dumb luck," I said. I don't know what it was I expected Toni to say. I don't think I expected her to do a fandango on the kitchen table just because I had the greatest lover who ever walked the face of this earth, but I certainly wasn't going to let her make me feel guilty. After all, it wasn't as though I'd been gloating, or lording it over her.

She knocked back the rest of her coffee as though it were a stiff drink, then set the cup back on the table, centering it precisely in front of her. "Then I take it," she said slowly, deliberately, "that you two are, as they say, an item."

"Yes, I guess we must be."

"Don't you know? Didn't you talk?"

"Not about Us with a capital *U* and our Future with a cap *F.* We didn't do that much talking at all, actually." I could see where her questions were leading, and I didn't like the direction, but I couldn't think what to do about it, either.

"This is going to change things, isn't it?"

"What do you mean?" I said. My voice sounded a bit too loud in my ears and my tone defensive. "Why should anything change?"

"Well . . . you know. I mean you're going to be spending a lot of your time with Ben . . . not that you shouldn't, of course you should, but . . . well, we have the film society series tickets, and the chamber opera and, you know . . ." Her eyes were so large, so lost, I felt a catch in my throat.

"Don't be such a goose," I said. "How long have we been best friends—seventeen years? That's a long time when you think about it. I've known you longer than anyone in my whole life. And we've always been closer than close. Why should that change just because I have a new fella?"

"Forget it." She gave me her usual shrug. "I guess I'm just being silly," she said.

I didn't for a minute believe she meant it. Desperate to change the subject, I said, "I'm starving. I wonder why sex always makes me hungry, and great sex makes me ravenous. Let's have boiled eggs and tons of bacon."

"I can't," she said. "I'm on a new diet."

"Since when?"

"Since yesterday, after work. I wandered into Bloomingdale's on the way home—you know, just to look around. And suddenly I felt this enormous pull sucking me, like an undertow, into one of the boutiques. It was so simple, but so gorgeous . . ."

"What was?"

"This scrumptious unitard. It has a V-front that's cut down to the bottom of the rib cage. Here." She patted her middle.

I didn't say a word. Not a single word. I didn't allow my features to betray any emotion known to man. I was rigid in my nothingness.

"It's a stirrup unitard, cotton and Lycra, or some such. And you've never seen such a blue. It's a deep, deeeeep, deeeeeeep blue they call midnight. Before I knew what had happened to me I was standing in front of a triple-mirror wearing this unitard."

"I hate triple-mirrors."

"You know what I looked like? I looked like fifteen grapefruits in a blue unitard."

"You're exaggerating."

"God, how I loathe triple-mirrors."

"You're not being sensible about this. Some people simply aren't meant to wear unitards. They're just not designed that way. Some people can sing counter-tenor, or dance in toe shoes, or whatever, others can't."

"You know how Ned's always pointing to people like Cher—with great bodies. When he saw Cher on the Oscars in that transparent dress he nearly fell through the television screen."

If I'd been Toni I'd cheerfully have throttled Ned, but then I'm not Toni.

"I wonder how long I'd have to live on brown rice and broccoli before I'd begin to look like Cher in that uni-tard?"

"There's nothing wrong with the way you look," I insisted, and I meant it. "You have a mesomorphic body type, that's all. And I'm not going to cheer you on from the sidelines while you turn yourself into a neurotic, self-loathing anorexic. The whole world loves Mari-lyn Horne, but you could never describe her as look-ing like a prepubescent string bean."

"Do you really think that, or are you just saying that to humor me?"

"Of course I mean it. It's not as though you're fat. You're not. You're ... rounded."

"You know," she said, "the one thing in the world I hate most is hips. Oh, well," she sighed, and dropped two slices of bread into the toaster, "pass the butter."

YOU CAN TELL A LOT about a man by the way he reacts to you the next time he sees you after the first time you've made love. Toni and I were wedged into the back of the elevator, waiting for the doors to close when Ben stepped in. He was holding a bunch of flowers. He smiled at me, over the heads of Lars and Paul, a flock of typists, and Mr. Grice and one of his cohorts from accounting. All the air leaked out of my lungs.

"Hi!" Toni said to Ben, a mischievous glint in her eye.

"Good morning," he said to Toni without taking his eyes from mine.

"Hello," I think I said.

"Can you drop down and have coffee with me around eleven?" Toni said to Ben. "I'll have the roughs for the Litton-Baird mystery ready for you to take a look at. I thought we'd use a big red firecracker on the cover."

"Sure," said Ben. He stared at me, his eyes soft. I wanted to stand on tiptoe and kiss the corners of his mouth where they curled up so slyly, so deliciously.

The elevator stopped. A couple of people got off, I think. Someone might have gotten on. The doors closed.

I smiled back at Ben, remembering everything, aching again for his touch. Toni said something about proofs, or progs, or some such. Ben grunted.

The doors opened again, and Toni got off. The doors closed, and as we rose I admired the exquisite design of Ben's ears. When the doors opened again, Ben and I walked as casually as strangers toward my office.

"Good morning," said Gudrun, glancing pointedly at the flowers in Ben's hand.

"'Morning," Ben and I mumbled in unison.

Walking that last fifteen feet to my office door was like crossing the endless wastes of the Sahara. Ben opened the door. We stepped inside. I closed it and leaned against it. I needed it for support because I thought my knees might buckle.

"For you," said Ben, holding the flowers between us.

"I guessed," I said, taking them—perky red tea roses in a damp, green paper cone.

We were fine until our hands touched, then it was as though we had never parted, as though we were once again making love on his creaking old sofa. We threw ourselves at each other as though we'd been separated by years, by miles, by clashing armies. We telescoped the reunion of a lifetime. He hugged me so fiercely, I dropped the flowers and buried both hands in his beautiful black hair.

"How," he murmured, "am I going to get through the day without making love to you?" He kissed me before I could answer, which was just as well, because I didn't have an answer; I'd been wondering the same thing.

Was what I felt more intense because we were, once again, engaging in decidedly extra-editorial activity on the Press premises at nine o'clock in the morning? Very possibly so. But as I stood there in Ben's arms, in my office, with Gudrun lurking outside, and all the busy business of the Press going on around us, I realized that what I felt for Ben was something entirely new to me: it was pure, unbridled lust. Lust the way men have always said they feel it, and few women have the guts to admit to. *I wanted Ben!* I wanted his kisses and caresses, the joy of his sucking mouth, his bold tongue, his gentle hands and clever fingers. I wanted to feel the weight of him pressing me down, the two of us sliding against each other, slithery with sweat. I wanted to feel him moving deep inside me, hard and silken. *I wanted Ben!*

"When?" he said.

"Tonight." I pressed two loving fingers against his lips, lips fuller and redder this morning, bruised from all our kissing. "Tonight, my darling."

"Promise?" he said, his tongue darting out to lick my fingers.

I slid my other hand down his long back and gave his beautiful backside a promising squeeze. That's when my phone started ringing, and Ben, disguising his excitement by taking off his jacket and carrying it over his arm in front of him, made his escape past the ever-vigilant Gudrun.

And that, more or less, was how nearly every morning started for us. As often as we could manage it, Ben or I would find some excuse to visit the other's office. An excuse with plausibility written all over it, or so we thought. I might rap on his door, for example, asking brightly, "Did you see this review?" My tone would be thoroughly conversational, my hands would be full of photocopies, and my voice pitched just loud enough for anyone passing in the hall behind me to hear. As soon as the door closed we'd fling ourselves at one another, kissing wildly for about two and a half minutes. Then we'd straighten our clothes and carry on as though nothing had happened.

In between these frantic encounters we got down to the business of being editors, which, we both agreed, is not unlike the never-ending labors of the mythical Sisyphus who forever struggled to heave a boulder to the very top of a mountain only to have it roll down just at the moment when he thought he had achieved the summit. There isn't an editor in the world who doesn't go home every night with a book-bag bulging with manuscripts and a heart brimming with good intentions. I know I did, and I know Ben did, because we usually met in the elevator. And perhaps a measure of how much we cared about our work is the fact that we did not spend every waking moment from dark till dawn in bed together. Most of our evenings were spent working. Sometimes Ben went out with Ross or his other friends, just as I spent evenings with Toni and our friends.

When we did come together, it was like a couple of runaway freight trains meeting head-on. We quickly discovered that we were incapable of behaving like other overworked people, sensible people, who contrive to relegate their sex lives to Wednesdays and Saturdays. We withdrew into our work, shoved our boulders up our private Alps, then rushed to each other's arms. It was all like those endless piano runs that hurry up and down the keyboard, thrilling arpeggios, advancing a bit more each time, but never resolving— passionate, blazing.

8

Liz

LOOKING BACK ON THEM, the next few weeks rushed us along as though we had a whirlwind at our backs. We were in a rage of love. Love that was nothing like the overwhelming passion you feel when you are twenty, when you believe—with all the naiveté of self-regarding youth—that love can never end. At our age we knew that everything ends, but that only made our moments together more precious, our passion more intensely felt.

Ben stopped bringing flowers to my office. Now he sent them. Masses of luscious pink roses with cards so sweet and soppy I've never even shown one to Toni. I began by tucking them into my wallet, but soon there were too many for that, so I carried only the first one and filed the others in my bottom drawer. Gudrun, of course, was tremendously excited by all the goings-on. She made it very plain that she thought I had lured this innocent lad—he's forty-two and so far from innocent as to make the *Kamasutra* read like a primer—into a low and vulgar relationship, while she, on the other hand, had clearly hoped to entice him into a mingling of souls on a higher plane. Gudrun's idea of a perfect evening with Ben would have been a joint workout with her personal trainer, followed by a reading from some minor German poet—in the original.

However, Ben and I were in complete agreement on what constituted a perfect evening: it was any evening that ended with the two of us in his bed. We found the time to go to plays and movies. We even went to poetry readings! And everywhere we went, we walked. First, to Mott Street in search of the elusive perfect dim sum; then, to the SoHo galleries to see the newest paintings. Then we'd walk some more. There was something mildly erotic in strolling together, arm in arm, our bodies moving rhythmically together—brushing, touching, coming apart, brushing, touching, coming apart. Just being together made the commonplace extraordinary. A shared hotdog, eaten in Central Park and spiced with love and kisses cannot be matched by the rarest dish eaten alone.

One night as we lay in his darkened bedroom, drifting together toward sleep, I gathered up my courage and asked him the question that had been in the back of my mind for so long.

"Why did you stop writing after one book?"

"It's the only book I've ever had in me. It wasn't as though I chose the subject. The subject chose me. Grabbed me by the throat, sat me down and made me write it. I didn't know it at the time. I thought I was writing it for myself and the guys I'd fought with in Viet Nam. But somewhere in the middle of the third draft I realized I was also writing it for my father. I worried about him a lot when I was a kid. He'd been in World War II, but he wouldn't talk to me about it, and he wouldn't talk to my mother. On Friday nights he'd go to the Vets' Post and drink beer with his buddies and come home when they closed the bar, blind drunk. On Saturday mornings he'd sit at the kitchen table red-eyed, his face gray and haunted and unshaven, drinking coffee. 'Why do you go?' my mother would ask him. 'Why do you go when it makes you so miserable?' 'Just to talk, Mary,' he'd always say. 'Just to talk.' What I understood from his silence was that civilians can never know what war is like unless it happens to them.

"By the time it was my turn to go in '67, my father was no longer alive to tell me, finally, what his war had been like—I knew it only from books. 'They never tell you what it was really like,' he always said. I was still in college—I could have gotten a deferment, but looking back, I think I wanted to go find out what it was really like. I was barely twenty. A kid. I wanted to know what the men like my father had experienced. It's hard to explain after all these years, but I really thought I wouldn't be a man until I experienced it, too."

His voice changed then, becoming deeper and at the same time lighter, and I knew he was not telling this story to me, he was telling it to himself. And I knew from the way he told it that he had told himself this same story many times before, but not for a very long time, and never to a woman who lay in his arms, loving him.

"In the beginning, in the rawness of our youth and our boundless ignorance, we believed ourselves invincible. After three weeks, the idea that we might survive was as utterly implausible as bad fiction. No one grows up faster than a raw recruit in battle. One day we were pinned down by a cross fire. We were waiting for an air strike to clear out the Viet Cong mortars so we could move up. The air strike didn't come. Some screwup. Chuff and I had dug ourselves a foxhole in a shellhole. Chuff was another grunt, just like me, but he had a theory about shells. Chuff thought they were like lightning, that they wouldn't strike twice in the same place. He'd already been in Nam for more than two hundred and fifty days. In those days, if you could make it to three hundred and sixty-five you could go home. I've read since that the army shrinks have figured out that the longest a man can stand to live in combat before he goes crazy is two hundred to two hundred and forty days.

"Chuff and I spent three days and nights squatting in that filthy, stinking foxhole, waiting for an air strike that never came. He told me how his whole platoon had been shot out from under him, how he was the only one left. It had happened only a week before I'd joined the unit. His hands shook, he chain-smoked, he had eight canteens clipped to his belt and all of them were full of booze. I don't think he'd been sober since it happened.

"For three days and three nights, we talked. Sometimes the mortars let up and we'd doze, but mostly we talked. About everything, everything but our fear of death. We talked about our lives back home, our families, the girls we'd known, the girls we'd like to know. We talked about our dreams, we even talked about God. But we never talked about fear.

"Finally, at dawn on the fourth day, the copters arrived and cleared out the VCs holding us pinned there, and the order came up to advance. There was still some sporadic fire, but not much, just enough to keep us low. We slithered forward on our bellies, maybe ten feet apart. Then there was this terrific detonation, and Chuff was gone. He'd crawled over a mine.

"So I wrote my novel to tell about all this. To tell what it was really like for Chuff, for me, for my father, and all the other grunts who fought in all the other wars."

"Do you have a copy? I'd like to read it."

"No, I don't have any copies. They were excess baggage I got rid of years ago. It's over now. It was a long, long time ago. Forget it."

How could I forget a thing like that? Ben had distilled all his pain into a single novel. Of course I couldn't forget it. "Have you forgotten it?" I said.

"It's not something you can forget, no matter how much you might want to, but I've stopped dreaming about it. I used to dream about it every night until they put up the wall, the memorial, in Washington. Finally, I went there, and I touched Chuff's name, and the dreams stopped."

We lay for a long time, holding each other in the dark.

9

Liz

I SUPPOSE IT WAS inevitable that our friends would begin to chafe. Toni's constantly reiterated phrase was, "I never see you anymore." Ross's, said Ben, was, "Where've you been keeping yourself?" We were both having trouble juggling our lives. One night, for example, I dashed home late from an author conference, showered with the speed of light and flew to my closet—I had promised to meet Ben at Bettina's for a quick bite before going on to Shea Stadium. He'd been trying for weeks to talk me into going to a baseball game with him. I was on my hands and knees trying to find my sneakers when Toni appeared in my bedroom doorway.

"Hi!" she said, leaning against the doorjamb and nibbling on a Cajun chicken leg. "I got so hungry I couldn't wait."

"There's a dustball in here devouring all my shoes."

"You'd better hurry. Curtain's at 7:30 p.m."

"It's eaten my sneakers. Have you seen my— Curtain? What curtain?"

"I thought you and I were going to Circle in the Square."

"I completely forgot. I made a date with Ben to go to a ball game."

"A ball game? You?"

"I'll call him and cancel. We can go another time."

"No, don't do that," she insisted. "Don't cancel on my account. I don't mind going alone. Really, I don't mind a bit."

"Are you absolutely sure?"

"Absolutely sure."

"Do you swear it?"

"No problem. I'll call Drew, maybe she'd like to go."

I felt like such a rat. I felt lower than low. The next day I sneaked out on my lunch hour and bought her three new blades for her Cuisinart. I didn't examine my motives, either. I just did it. A bruised conscience is harder to live with than an aching tooth. You can fix a tooth.

IT WAS ONLY A DAY or two later when Ben put his head around my office door. I blew him a kiss and waved him to a chair. I was in the middle of a call from Dan Neal— one of my more skittish authors.

"I'm...ah...working on something...ah... new," said Dan.

"Tell me all about it," I said.

Ben dropped a paper bag on my desk and sat down across from me, stretching his long legs out in front of him and propping one ankle on top of the other. He rubbed his head against the back of the chair and watched me with half-closed eyes.

"I suppose you'd...call it an anti-logical form of storytelling..."

Ben's eyes said, *Let's go to bed.*

"...one that marries drastic invention...and whimsical speculation...with details that are...well...utterly commonplace..."

Dan Neal's voice trailed away, and what with Ben's eyes sending me love messages while I admired, for the thousandth time, the line of his jaw, it took me a moment or two to sort out this minimalist gibberish.

"That's not for you, Dan," I said finally. "Your roots go back to Faulkner. Why try so hard to do something so alien when you write so superbly in your own idiom?"

"I do?"

"Beyond question you do." Writers, like actors, require buckets of reassurance, and we, editors, are keepers of the magic well. It's all part of the job. Show me a writer who doesn't doubt himself, and I'll show you a hack.

"How are you coming with...um..." I thought furiously—what was the working title of Dan's Civil War saga? "...with your script," I finished up lamely. I'd been promising myself for years that one day I'd keep just that sort of information, including names of current mates or lovers, children, etc., on my Rolodex, but somehow I'd never gotten around to it.

"I'm in the middle of chapter six," said Dan with a hopeful lilt that belied the terror I knew must have driven him to believe he should try something new.

I moved Ben's bag aside and consulted my calendar. "Why don't you come in around 4:30 this afternoon. We'll talk about it."

"Talk?" He sounded frightened.

"You know, schmooze a little. Maybe between us we can figure out what the problem is."

"I'd have to take the train," he said, as though this meant organizing a safari with native bearers and elephant guns. Dan lived in Connecticut. He loathed any form of travel.

"I'll see you at 4:30," I said and hung up. "What's in the bag?" I asked Ben.

"Lunch. I hate waiting until evening to see you. You're either working through lunch, or out with an author or an agent, or nibbling salads down in the art department with Toni. I mentioned it to Ross this morning and he counseled the direct approach. So here I am, bearing lunch." He drew his chair up beside me. "Kiss me, Shweetheart." Ben always says this in his Humphrey Bogart-Sam Spade voice. And it always makes me giggle—he's such a rotten mimic that he's endearing when he tries to be corny.

"Do you discuss me with Ross?" The idea gave me a prickly feeling.

"Sometimes," he said, busying himself pulling sandwiches and pickles from the bag. "Do you talk to Toni about me?"

"Naturally," I said. "She's my best friend."

He looked up sharply. "What do you tell her?"

"I tell her how much I adore you," I said without missing a beat. Men, of course, would die of embarrassment if they knew how women really talk about them.

"Ben, darling," I continued, not wanting to lose momentum. "When am I going to meet this Ross you talk about all the time? You say he's your best friend, but he's always in the background. Don't you think we should meet?"

He chewed thoughtfully on his roast beef sandwich. "How about a double date?" he said. He put his sandwich down and drank some coffee. "Why didn't I think of it before? Ross is so miserable since his girl ran out. And I think Toni's great. You know I think she's great. If I like her, Ross is bound to like her. How about next Saturday night? What do you say?"

"I'll ask her," I said. "But I can't promise anything. Toni's been wrapped up in this actor for so long, I don't know if she'd agree to go out with anyone else."

"This wouldn't mean anything. It would just be an evening out with a couple of friends."

"Toni has some very strong feelings about what she calls loyalty, but I'll ask her," I said.

Ben

I LEFT LIZ to her pile of manuscripts, made what I thought was a pretty good end run around the everlurking Gudrun and got on the horn to Ross.

"How's it going?" I said.

"It's not good and true, Beniamino," said Ross. "The writing, I mean. Haven't been able to write since my woman left me."

"I've got the cure for that. It's time you met Liz. How about spending an evening with Liz and me and her roommate, Toni? The one I told you about. The art director here."

"There is no luck in anything anymore," said Ross. "I think my jade plant is dying."

"An evening out is just what the doctor ordered," I insisted.

"One day, your plants will die, too, Ben. There is no luck on this island. Everything dies."

"Cut that out!" I pleaded. When Ross is crossed in love, he slides into his Hemingway mode, which always sets my teeth on edge. "I'll pick you up Saturday night at seven. And don't wear your plaid jacket."

"What's wrong with my plaid jacket?"

"I hate that jacket."

"It was your jacket. You gave it to me."

"I hated it when it was my jacket. I'll see you at seven."

Liz

TONI WAS SLICING baby eggplants when I got home from work. I poured myself a glass of wine, sat down at the kitchen table and kicked off my shoes.

"Have you ever wondered," I said, wiggling my toes gratefully, "why it is that no matter how much you spend on a pair of shoes they never give you more pleasure than that delicious moment when you take them off?"

"That," said Toni waving her knife, "is one of life's great imponderable questions." She arranged the slices on a cookie sheet and salted them. "Some questions will never be answered, even by the greatest philosophers. *Is it possible to spend too much for a really good pair of shoes?* is right up there with, *Is the universe expanding, or is the universe contracting? And what is a black hole?*" She set a cutting board and a weight on the eggplant slices and sat down, a glass of wine in her hand.

"Ben has this friend named Ross."

"So I've heard," she said. "Have you met him?"

"Not yet. He's a good writer."

"I know he is. *And* his last book hung in there on the bestseller list for more than a year. Mr. Pomfret must be licking his chops in anticipation. I can't remember the last time the Press had a bestseller that lasted longer than a thunderstorm in July."

I could have named several, but I thought it more prudent not to mention them. "Ben says Ross is awfully down right now since his girlfriend left him...Ben thought, that is, we thought it might . . ."

"Are you trying to arrange a double date? You know what I think about double dates—they're about as much fun as a spoon-and-egg race and just as embarrassing. Besides, you know I don't date anyone but Ned. We have an agreement, Ned and I—"

"This wouldn't be a date," I said. "Not a real date. Not a *date* date."

"Just an intimate little evening for four. I don't think so."

"I for one am dying to meet this Ross."

"By his friends shall ye know him?"

"Something of that, I suppose. Ben says he's a marvelous guy."

"He would say that, wouldn't he? This Ross is supposed to be his best friend. What else would you expect him to say? 'I've got this buddy who's a real drag. How about fixing him up with your best friend?'"

I let it rest there while I took a fast shower. I was back in the kitchen in time to top the now fried eggplant slices with our secret sauce of sun-dried tomatoes, garlic and fresh basil, and cubes of goat cheese, before popping them into the oven to bake.

"Ben says Ross is a big, big guy." I was leading from my strongest suit. I happened to know that Toni's sexual fantasies always involved big, muscular men. Ned wasn't big. He was tall, but there was no real meat on him. Toni once confided that sex with Ned was like going to bed with a double-jointed paper clip.

"How big?" Her tone implied I might be trying to fob off a mere mortal on her.

"Broad. Tall. I don't know. Ben says Ross looks like he should be snowshoeing through a forest with an ax on his shoulder with a blue ox snorting at his heels."

"That big?"

"Hmm." I could only hope Ben hadn't been pulling my leg and Ross would turn out to be a shrimp.

"When?"

"Next Saturday." Then I played my trump card. "Ben and I thought we'd like to go to Marguerite's." Marguerite's has been *the* French restaurant since it opened six months ago. It is supposed to be booked almost a year in advance. "Ben, it seems, knows Marguerite— through Natasha Fleer, the sculptor."

"This isn't going to *mean* anything," she said.

"Of course not. We're just four people spending the evening together."

"And you won't breathe a word of this to Ned."

"Cross my heart and hope to die."

Toni AND I arrived at the restaurant only a few minutes before Ben and Ross. We had, of course, expected them to pick us up at our apartment, but just when we'd begun to wonder where they were, Ben phoned to say they'd be delayed—something about a jacket that I didn't quite get—and would we go ahead so as not to lose the table. The moment we walked into Marguerite's I could see Toni approved. The kind of taste and wit which Toni believes to be the exclusive birthright of every Frenchwoman was evident everywhere—in the semicircular banquettes of deepest aubergine, set against peaches-and-cream walls; in the dozen or so gold-framed *Directoire* portrait heads, none larger than a page of manuscript; in the thin-stemmed crystal and heavy table silver flanking black plates on palest peach-colored linen. Very low-key classic jazz murmured in the background.

We were busily approving of Marguerite's style when Ben and Ross came in. Ben had said that Ross was big. He was big. What Ben had not said was that Ross was beautiful. Perhaps Ben didn't know this. It may be that men cannot see this kind of beauty in each other, or perhaps they choose not to see it. I suppose it's also possible that only women perceive the beauty in a face like Ross's, but to my not unpracticed eye he was beautiful in the way antique statues are beautiful. Every woman he had ever known must have told him so, but it was obvious that Ross had never believed them. He was absolutely unselfconscious and without any affectation whatsoever. Toni, I think, was quite prepared to like him. She has always had a soft spot for flat blond hair, sky-blue eyes, high, sharp cheekbones and Ross's kind of modest smile. And I, for my part, was sure I'd like him—after all, he was Ben's best friend. What better recommendation could there be?

Once the introductions had been made and we were seated on an aubergine banquette of our own, I said to Ben, "What was all that about a jacket?"

"Nothing important." He pressed his knee meaningfully into my leg. "Let's all have a drink, shall we?" Ross raked him a sky-blue glare.

"Yes, by all means," I twittered in my best social small-talk manner. "Do let's order drinks, Ben, darling."

While Ben dispatched a waiter with our orders, Ross turned to Toni and said, "Do you know anything about jade plants?"

"Only that you're supposed to be careful about overwatering them," she said.

Ross took out his wallet, extracted a snapshot and handed it to Toni. "What do you think? Does that look overwatered?"

"Hard to tell from a picture." She gave it back to him.

Ross looked at me, but I shook my head. "I'm not a plant person."

He turned back to Toni. "It was Iris's. My girl's. She left me."

"I'm sorry," said Toni.

"Thank you." He stared at his snapshot in silence. Then he said, "She left me for a photographer. She's a fashion model." He slid another picture from his wallet and passed it to Toni.

Toni studied the snapshot, then Ross. "Androgyny's a very in look these days," she said, pointing to one of the figures.

"That's not Iris, that's the S.O.B. she ran off with. That one on the end is Iris." He stabbed at the picture with his finger.

If there was one single moment when the evening started to go off the rails, this was it. Why didn't I step in and say something? Why didn't Ben? We were mesmerized. It was like watching the Titanic approaching the iceberg.

"That's Iris?" said Toni, squinting at the photograph. "She looks like Katherine Hepburn in *Christopher Long*."

"That's *Strong. Christopher Strong.* 1933."

"I'm sure you're mistaken," she said icily. "It's *Christopher Long*."

"It's 'Strong.' I know it's 'Strong,' because old movies have been a hobby of mine since I was nine years old."

"Have they really? If movies were such a passion of yours you'd know it was 'Long.'"

"'Strong,'" he repeated through clenched teeth. Then before she could reply he said, "Who wrote the screenplay for *Strangers on a Train?*"

"Raymond Chandler," said Toni with a look that said, *You have to throw harder than that to catch me out.* "Who played Edwina Brown in *National Velvet?*" she snapped back.

"Ha!" said Ross with a snort. "Angela Lansbury." I could see him preparing to slam another ace over the net.

"Aperitif?" interrupted our waiter who looked distressingly like a French count, slumming. "I believe *mesdames* ordered an aperitif."

I smiled my gratitude up at him, and blessed him and all his issue unto the tenth generation. Ben seemed paralysed. Had he had some premonition of disaster? Was Ross always like this, I wondered, or was there something in Toni that brought out his contentious side? Toni, on the other hand, was hardly behaving like Gloria Gracious.

Ross narrowed his eyes at Toni. "Who danced the roles of Columbine and Harlequin in Chaplain's *Lime-light?*"

Toni all but sneered. "Melissa Heyden and André Eglevsky."

It was as though they were trapped in a terrible compulsion. Nothing could stop them. Over the mussel salads Toni looked as if she might start up again. In desperation, I brought Ben back to life with a wickedly hard pinch, and for a while the two of us talked, haltingly, about the off-Broadway season. Our voices sounded high and nervous, but we slogged dutifully on. Ross and Toni glowered at each other like a pair of Russian chess masters brooding over their next fifteen moves.

"Who made her film debut in *Miracle on 34th Street?*" said Toni over her roast rabbit with lentils.

"I've seen that," said Ben.

"I missed it," I said. We both knew it was hopeless.

"Thelma Ritter," said Ross. "Who played Rosa Klebb in *From Russia with Love?*"

"Lotte Lenya." Toni stared thoughtfully at her empty plate. I could practically hear the cogs and gears racing in her head. In the middle of her mango sorbet she looked up at Ross and said, *"The Thin Man—"*

Ross jumped right in. "William Powell and Myrna Loy, 1934. Based on the novel by Dashiell Hammett."

"That's so obvious, it's grotesque. That's not what I wanted to ask."

"What did you want to ask?"

"Who was the cinematographer?"

Ross didn't reply until he and Ben dropped us at our apartment. There was no question of asking them up.

The last thing I heard as we got out of the taxi was Ross calling after Toni, "Howe! Howe! James Wong Howe!"

We crossed the lobby to the sound of Toni breathing angrily through her nose. She stabbed the call-button and said, "I don't want to talk about tonight. Not ever. I have never in my entire life met such a pure, such an unmitigated, unregenerated, swelled-headed, horse's ass. I wouldn't touch a book design for that man if he were the last writer on earth."

"One of these days he'll be giving Ben his latest manuscript."

"When the specs come down, I'll turn him over to one of the new kids. Pomfret won't care. Probably won't even know the difference. I don't ever want to see that man again."

"He's awfully good-looking."

"I never noticed."

10

Liz

SOMETIMES YOU'RE SO caught up in the knotted skein of
your own problems that it's impossible to see where the
loose thread is, where to begin pulling so that you can
begin to unravel the impossible tangle that has become
your life.

It wasn't long after our disastrous double date that
Toni and I met our friends Drew and Christine for dinner at our favorite Japanese restaurant. The four of us
usually got together every month or so to pig out on
twenty-seven varieties of sushi, mountains of pickled
ginger and oceans of hot saki and green tea. Drew, who
was a few years younger than Toni and I, began her
professional life as a starry-eyed crime reporter. She
once confessed to me that her career in crime hadn't
lasted through her first assignment. When a homicide
cop showed her her first victim, she took one look and
threw up all over the cop's shiny black shoes. Then she
wangled a transfer to the science desk—she'd been a
whiz at college physics—a field where no one ever got
sick. Before long she was editing nonfiction for Wob-
bleday.

Chris was an art director who left publishing to join
one of the creative teams at Cunningham and Fitzger-
ald, the ad agency. The only one of us who had been

married, Chris wore her divorce decree like a battle ribbon until she discovered health, and the place in her life once occupied by her husband was filled with low-impact aerobics.

When the hot-towels had been taken away, we began catching each other up on what we'd been doing, and sharing all the gossip—good, bad and indifferent. Drew was all excited about a new author she'd taken on.

"He's brilliant," she said, almost belligerently. "He's done an absolutely riveting book on the Heisenberg Uncertainty Principle."

"Do I detect a wee bit of defensiveness here?" said Toni.

"Has he asked you out?" asked Chris.

I could see the answer in her eyes. "How old is he?"

Drew sipped her saki with theatrical nonchalance. "Older," she said carelessly. Her cuticles suddenly demanded her instant attention.

"Forty?"

"Fifty?"

"Fifty-five?"

"Something like that," she said.

"Father figure, father figure," chanted Chris, stroking an imaginary goatee. Chris, who once had had a sensational affair with a Freudian analyst, was our self-proclaimed resident expert in these matters.

"Rubbish!" said Drew with a barely suppressed giggle. "My father was a bandy-legged Irishman no taller than my mother's broom. Pavel is six feet tall, with a fuzzy brown beard. He looks like a giant teddy bear in red suspenders. And yes, we've been out together. Twice. He took me to the Haydon Planetarium to look at the stars, and he took me to the Russian Tea Room."

"I love the Russian Tea Room," said Chris.

"I can't imagine going out with someone that old," said Toni.

"The difference in our ages just doesn't seem to be a factor," said Drew. "It never enters into anything we do or talk about. I'll tell you what I like best about Pavel—he can surprise me. I am so tired of predictable men. I never know what Pavel's going to say next. He makes me feel so alive.... I used to dream about what it would be like to know a man who knows things I don't know, sings songs I've never heard, sees his world in a way that's new to me. If my age doesn't bother him, why should his bother me?"

No one had an answer to that, so we ate our sushi in silence until Chris said, "I wish you'd consider aerobics. It's done so much for me." Given a chance, Chris will prattle on for hours about her aerobics instructor who is called Memmo—as in "I'll send you one"—but whose name is really Agamemnon, as in the Trojan War. Sensing Chris was about to start up, Drew asked me about Ben, but I didn't really want to talk about him. I think I was afraid I might jinx everything if I said too much. It wasn't until dinner was nearly over and we four were happily munching on pineapple wedges and melon that Toni asked if anyone had talked to Sandra lately. She and Bill were getting married in July.

"I had lunch with her last week," said Chris. "She looked like grim death."

"Do you know where they're going on their honeymoon?" asked Toni.

"Tahiti," said Drew. "When I ran into her at the Pottery Barn yesterday I hardly recognized her. She's lost about twenty pounds. Her hair was hanging in strings, and she has some kind of rash all over her arms . . ."

"Isn't it awful?" said Chris. "It's stress. We had a long talk about it over lunch. Her mother is driving her crazy. She's so stressed out, she's a wreck. I told her what she needs is to run off with Bill and go on her honeymoon now and get married later. If I decide to marry Memmo, I promise you, we'll do it without mothers, I swear. Judge's chambers, no relatives. Only friends."

"When did you get so serious about this Memmo?"

"Last Thursday. I ran into a woman I used to work for. She'd just retired, and she was walking on air. She told me she'd closed on a house in some eensy-weensy village in France. She says the house has an absolutely glorious garden. Can you believe it? Selling an apartment in New York to go and live in the boonies in France?"

"I think that's wonderful," said Toni. "It sounds like—"

"Heaven," I said.

"You two are such besotted Francophiles, you're missing the point," said Chris, stabbing at a piece of pineapple. "The point is, she's going to live all by herself. Alone. 'I'm going to spend the rest of my life painting,' she said. I tried to imagine it—I really did, and the more I thought about it, the more the idea made me . . . well, I guess the word is *queasy*. It's like that feeling you get when you give a dollar to some poor pathetic bag lady and all the time you're thinking, Oh, god, that could so easily be me—"

"Do you feel that way, too?"

"That's what I always think . . ."

"And I thought I was the only one..."

"Well, that's when I decided it was time to take a closer look at Memmo..."

"I don't believe it," said Toni, her voice fluting with exasperation. "You sound like Linus in a panic because he's alone without his security blanket. Is that reason enough to get married? Living alone is better than hooking up to some guy just because you can't stand making toast for one every morning."

"But you don't live alone, do you?" snapped Chris.

Drew looked over at me. "What do you think, Liz? Would you marry for companionship?"

Toni studied her plate, her lower lip caught between her teeth.

"I don't know," I said. "Maybe I'm the last of the incurable romantics, but I've honestly never imagined marrying for anything but love. But ten years, fifteen years from now..." I glanced around the group. "Which of us can predict what she might do?"

Chris said, "But what about you and this Ben you've been seeing?"

"Ben and I haven't gotten that far. We're just getting to know each other. Talking about things like commitment, like marriage is a long, long way off."

"Really?" said Chris. "I take that as a sign that you're really serious about him. Subconsciously, of course. Now, I always start considering marriage about ten minutes into the first date. Do you suppose that's why none of the men in my life have ever quite measured up? Maybe it's just that I'm older than you. I'm sure I'm older than you. I'm older than everyone I know. I'm the only one who can still remember when there were soap operas on radio. How old are you, Liz?"

Drew smiled sweetly at Chris. "Was that before Grant took Lee's surrender at Appomattox?"

"We're both thirty-five," said Toni with a weird little laugh. "Do you know what that makes us? That makes us three years older than the Marschallin in *Der Rosenkavalier.*"

Chris wagged a finger. "Wait a minute, don't tell me. I remember. She's the one who takes a young lover. Right? But I thought she was supposed to be old. Not as old as *Harold and Maud,* but you know, old."

"*Experienced* would be a better word for her," said Toni. "Worldly is even better. Can you believe it? In 1910, when the opera was written, a married woman of thirty-two was thought of as on the brink of middle age. She wasn't old, but she was teetering. And here I am three years past the brink already. Just the idea makes me feel creepy."

"I've always imagined the Marschallin would go on taking lovers for years and years and years," I said. "But none, of course, would ever be so sweet, so bittersweet as her young Octavian."

"He was only seventeen," said Toni.

"Is that all he was?" said Chris with a long slow sigh. "Seventeen . . . Imagine what it would be like to have a seventeen-year-old lover."

"No thanks," said Drew. "I had a seventeen-year-old lover. He was dumb and clumsy, and I was scared stiff."

"That's because you were seventeen," said Toni. "Kids that age don't know the difference between making love and opening an oyster."

"Men are always taking younger and younger lovers," said Chris. "These days there's an inverse relationship between a man's age and his girlfriend's, or haven't you noticed. Seventeen's too young for me. I wouldn't want to have to teach him everything. But twenty-two would be a good age. Yes, I'd enjoy having a boy of twenty-two for a lover . . ." Chris surveyed us with half-closed eyes, a seraphic smile on her face.

I didn't want a stripling lover, I wanted Ben. I was beginning to feel like the Marschallin, and I wasn't crazy about the feeling. There's an aria in the opera where she admits that she sneaks around the house in the dark stopping the clocks. Time was running out for me, too. Was I going to end up like the Marschallin with a teenage lover who falls for the first young thing he meets? Would I end up like Drew, with a man nearly twice my age? Or like Chris, scheming for a marriage with her aerobics instructor?

And what about my best friend? Was I going to be able to have a relationship with Ben without irrevocably damaging my friendship with Toni? There are so many different kinds of love. I suppose it's one of the unavoidable ironies of true friendship that all who love must live with divided hearts.

THAT NIGHT, as I always do, I reached for the topmost book on the never-diminishing heap that fills my nightstand. It was Ben's novel that had worked its way to the top. I felt ambushed and nearly put it back on the bottom. I'd been avoiding it like a booby trap ever since I'd found it, a shopworn remainder, in a dusty corner of the Strand bookstore. I wanted to read it, and yet I didn't want to read it. Finally, I made a bargain with myself—*just a couple of chapters, just enough to see what it's like*. I stuffed an extra pillow behind my head and started in.

I have read some pretty strong and affecting stuff in my day. I do, after all, think of myself as a hard-bitten fiction editor who has read it all from brutalized childhoods to a hundred other varieties of fictional mayhem. But I read Ben's book, and I wept. Not only for the wrenching personal tragedies of his war, but for the pain that had driven him to write it. It was not a great book, but it was a moving book, an honest book, one that forced the reader to confront his soldiers' realities of horror, fear, and loss. Yet, miraculously, it was not bitter. It held out the possibility that man might be perfectable after all. As old-fashioned as the idea might be to many, by the time I finished Ben's book he had convinced me of its truth.

It was five o'clock in the morning when I closed the cover. By then I was sitting at the kitchen table, drinking black coffee. There are moments, I believe, when a woman should act on her instincts. This was one of those moments. I called Ben.

"Grumph . . ." said a voice that could only be Ben's.

"Darling, it's Liz."

"Hmm?"

"Wake up!"

"I'm awake. Wide awake." A very long pause followed. "Who did you say this is?"

"It's me. Liz."

"What's wrong? Is anything wrong? Are you all right? Are you hurt? In jail? What's going on?"

"Darling, I'm fine. Just fine."

"Then why do you sound like you're crying? Are you really okay?"

"I just wanted to tell you I've been up all night reading your book."

"Oh."

"You should be very proud of it, Ben."

"Where, in the name of heaven, did you manage to dig up a copy?"

"At the Strand. I love you, Ben. That's all I wanted to say. I love you."

MY PHONE WAS ALREADY ringing when I walked into my office. "Darling!" drawled Gillian Ypes, "I have the most tremendous news. Richard's back. Can you believe it? He's back. He came swaggering in last night with all his buttons popping."

"Do you mean you've taken him back?"

"But he wasn't having an affair, darling. Truly. All those afternoons when I thought he was off with some doe-eyed ingenue, he was auditioning for television commercials. He didn't want me to know. He made Frank swear he wouldn't tell me. Isn't that just like Richard? Now he's going to make himself stinking rich, darling. He's going to be the spokesman, the image, for the What'sit—that new luxury car—I forget what it's called, but apparently it's Detroit's answer to the Rolls-Royce Corniche."

"But that's marvelous."

"Isn't it? Frank even managed to sign them to a three-year contract. Just think of the residuals! I never really believed the boy had it in him. Anyway, Richard and I are leaving for the Riviera tomorrow. Isn't that delicious? Two weeks of location shooting. I'll send you a card."

The next call was from Toni, from her studio downstairs. "Have you heard the latest?" Toni is the acknowledged expert on Press gossip. "The talking drums say there was some kind of screwup in the computer lists that were sent to the bindery. Almost all the shipments were either incomplete or over-count.

"Oh, no . . ." *Here we go again*, I thought. *It's starting again.*

"Talking drums say more. Entire sets of author-corrected galleys have disappeared over in nonfiction. What do you say to that?"

"I don't know. Maybe it's time to update our résumés."

Two hours later Mr. Pomfret walked into my office saying, "What do you make of all these so-called accidents, Miss Crosby?"

"I don't think it's just malicious mischief."

"Nor do I. Someone's apparently out to destroy the Press by destroying our reputation. Have you any thoughts on the matter?"

"Only that I can't imagine who'd want to do such a thing. I thought at first we'd been having a run of bad luck."

"That was naive of you," he said. "There's a sinister motive behind this. I came to ask you to keep your eyes and ears open. If anything further happens, you must tell me immediately. Do not discuss this with anyone—rumor is so dangerous—and this is the time for damage control. Let's hope it's not too late. I want to assure you I have already taken steps."

"Taken steps?"

"Exactly."

When I tried to talk to Ben about it that night, all he would say was, "Pomfret's taken steps. Keep your eyes open."

11

Liz

I ADORED WAKING UP in Ben's bed on Sunday mornings. I absolutely wallowed in the sensuous luxury of knowing that somewhere, not too far away, that gorgeous man, who had devoted the best part of the previous night to making the most delicious love, was now out in his kitchen trying very hard not to burn the toast. Dishes rattled. The teakettle whistled for attention. Somewhere, a radio sang softly to itself.

"Ben," I'd call. "Are you bringing coffee?" Of course he was bringing coffee. In my experience, men always brought you breakfast in bed on the very first Sunday. Sometimes this attentiveness would last as long three weeks. After that you'd better be prepared to get it yourself, or go without. But one of the wonderful things about Ben was that he and I had been lovers for more than a month and he still brought me breakfast in bed on Sunday mornings. And, perfect lover that he was, he brought not one but two copies of the *New York Times* so that we could prop ourselves up amongst the pillows, drink coffee and dawdle as long as we wanted to over the sections we liked best.

Equally important, we didn't have to fight over whose turn it was to do the crossword puzzle. I used a red, felt-tip pen. Ben used a number-two pencil and then swore because the letters were so pale. I rewrote in blue, if I made a mistake. Ben said this was messy. He erased. I complained that he was covering the sheets with eraser crumbs. This was one of the few areas of serious disagreement on which we had yet to work out a compromise. I believe that it is on matters such as these that relationships founder. Not politics, not interpretations of varieties of religious experience, but whether or not your mate scatters eraser crumbs all over the conjugal couch.

Ben would enter the bedroom with the breakfast tray held high. His face would still be stubbly, his hair tousled. Because he'd filled the orange juice glasses too full, he was balancing the tray with the concentration of a ten-year-old building a house of cards. I'd sit up against the pillows and pull the sheet up to my throat and tuck it under my arms. I'm told the world is full of women who are perfectly comfortable sitting around stark naked while they breakfast with their lovers. I am not one of them. Nor do I enjoy the feel of toast crumbs all over my breasts. I much prefer to breakfast with my chest covered—of course there was the morning when Ben spread marmalade . . . but that was another time.

Ben's breakfast tray was the sensible kind—large, with sturdy legs that won't collapse unexpectedly. It was enameled a gentle ivory, not glaring white, and delicately adorned with Beatrix Potter's sort of morning glorys. No man would ever buy such a tray for himself. It could only have been bought for him by a woman. I knew better than to quiz him about its origins.

Gingerly, he would set the tray over my lap, drop his robe onto the floor as unselfconsciously as a boxer, and slide in beside me with elaborate care, one eye on the orange juice. We'd kiss, and Ben would say, as he always said to me after the first kiss of the day, "Good morning, sweet love." Surely it is one of the mysteries of love, that words so simple could so completely disarm a woman's heart. Well, *this* woman's heart. I always wanted that kiss to go on forever. And it did last a gratifyingly long time, during which Ben, not constrained as I was by the tray over my knees, invariably slipped the sheet away from my breasts and dallied there. Why did I thrill to the feel of his stubbly cheeks on my breasts, but hate toast crumbs? Another of love's mysteries.

With the tray placed carefully between us, we breakfasted, read the paper, did our crosswords with our puzzles propped against our knees, and generally enjoyed the morning. Later, with the tray on the floor, we made slow, languorous love amid the toast and eraser crumbs. I liked a little nap then. As always, I woke to find Ben showered, shaved and dressed and sitting on the edge of the bed tying his shoes.

"Darling," I said, wrapping my arms around his waist and squeezing as hard as I could, "I don't know why I love you. But do I love you!" I knew as I said this that all lovers say the same thing, and that it is never strictly true, but a game we all play.

The truth was that I knew exactly why I loved Ben. He was wise, he was funny, he was gentleness itself; he was thoughtful and kind, attentive, generous to the proverbial fault. I know these sound like the virtues of a Boy Scout, but in those days of greed and glitz and tawdry glamour, these were virtues for a woman to fall in love with. So I clung to Ben as he sat on the edge of the bed, pressed my lips against his shining pink ear, and told him I adored him, and he hugged me back, his lips against my throat, murmuring words of love. I sighed happily. There had never, in the history of the world, been a man as wonderful as Ben. Take the week before, for example.

We met at the watercooler where I was trying to wash down aspirins with paper-thimbles of water. I had dragged myself into work with an awful case of cramps. I felt hideous, and I know I must have looked like something out of Poe's *The Mask of the Red Death.*

"Are you all right?" said Ben. "You look a little off-color."

"Among the cognoscenti my color is called 'sick-green.' I have cramps." I didn't see any point in being coy about it. If cramps are one of the bitterer facts of life for women, why shouldn't our lovers know about them? "I feel absolutely awful. I'm all tied up in knots, and I think my head might just explode."

Now this is the moment when other men would run for the hills, but not Ben. He touched my face, and looked at me as compassionately as he must have looked at his wounded buddies. "Why did you come in to work? You shouldn't be here. Let me take you home."

"I'll be okay. I'm only dying."

"Then let me help."

"Help?" If women have anything to say about it, the person who comes up with a cure for menstrual cramps will be nominated simultaneously for sainthood and the Nobel Prize and receive both. But before I could tell him this, an awful spasm twisted through me.

"Come along," said Ben as soon as I could straighten up. He hustled me down the hall to his office, and sat me down on the sofa, *our* sofa, saying, "Don't move!" and left. I heard him tell his secretary to hold all calls for half an hour, and a moment later he was back with a mug of black coffee. From the back of a file drawer he brought out a bottle. "Navy rum," he said, pouring a whopping dollop into the coffee. "Miraculous stuff."

"I can't drink that," I protested. "Not in the morning. At the office. Ben, I haven't even had breakfast. I'll be sick."

"Drink," he said, sitting down beside me and forcing the mug into my unwilling hands. "All of it. It's medicine."

I drank and shuddered. It tasted absolutely vile.

"All of it," he repeated.

Even as I finished the mug I felt a buzzing warmth spreading out from my stomach all the way to my fingers and toes. Tiny glowworms of warmth glimmered along my veins.

"Now," he said, "lean back, close your eyes and relax."

I didn't feel like arguing.

Ben put one arm around me, and I leaned back against his shoulder. Very, very gently, with a sweet circular motion, Ben massaged my knotted tummy. He did this tenderly and tirelessly for twenty minutes, and all the while he murmured softly, "Relax...let go...relax...let go..."

One by one the knots fell open, the spasms stilled. I was nearly asleep when I heard him say, more to himself than to me, "I think I could stand anything but to see you in pain." Then he kissed my listening ear and cuddled me in his arms, and I knew I could never love anyone as much as I loved Ben at that moment.

But now he was sitting on the edge of the bed and I thought I loved him more than ever as he whispered in my ear, "You just love me because I plied you with rum last week."

In answer I started nibbling on his earlobe.

"Sweetheart," he said, drawing back. "I have to go now. I'm meeting Ross for breakfast at Mona's Acapulco—" he checked his watch, "—in about six minutes. Do you want to come along?"

Of course I said no. A woman should always allow her lover time to spend "with the guys." It doesn't matter whether he's the president of a Fortune 500 company, or a pipefitter—men need to bond. We women bond, too, of course, but in a different way. With men it's a much more primal, tribal thing, I think—a throwback to hunting and gathering.

"Will you be here when I get back?" he asked, pulling on his jacket. "Or, are you doing something with Toni?" He sounded just a tad resentful.

"No, we're not doing anything. Toni has a date with Ned, I think. And I have a ton of work to get through before tomorrow."

He took me in his arms one last time, and the kisses he left with me were scented with soap and after-shave and tasted of cinnamon toothpaste.

As soon as I heard the door close, I pulled on his robe, picked up the tray from the floor and carried it out to the kitchen. This was no more than an alcove just off his book-lined living room. Ben's was beyond question a bachelor's apartment. It was small, simply furnished and felt comfortably snug in the way a well-fitted sloop feels snug. His living room had two leather chairs and a sofa the color of milk chocolate, a long teakwood coffee table that was nearly hidden beneath a drift of books, and a large, cluttered desk piled high with scripts and more books. His bathroom had the same snug, ship-at-sea quality. His shower head was the pulsing kind that feels so terrific when you get in knowing your back is covered with eraser crumbs.

Toni always said there are two kinds of women—those who look behind other people's shower curtains, and those who can't go into a strange bathroom without peeking into the medicine cabinet. I loved Ben's medicine cabinet. It was so basic and at the same time so defining. So Ben. So male. There were only three shelves. On the top shelf was a cobalt-blue bottle of Vicks, two gray plastic containers containing, between them, about nine miles of cinnamon-flavored dental floss, and a box of Q-tips. When I asked him what he did with Q-tips he said he dipped them in alcohol to clean the heads on his tape deck. I thought he used them on his ears and wouldn't admit it. Beside the Q-tips was a tiny orange tin of Tiger Balm and an immaculate comb and brush. On the second shelf he kept bandages, razor blades, two pieces of styptic pencil in a cloudy plastic tube, an optimistically generous supply of condoms, and a bottle of after-shave.

The bottom shelf held two tubes of cinnamon toothpaste, his deodorant, shaving cream, nail clipper, and a bottle of aspirin. His toothbrushes hung from a fancy high-tech Swedish toothbrush holder glued to the tile just above the sink. His razor, which had a heavy silver handle engraved with his initials—undoubtedly a gift, perhaps from the woman who'd given him the breakfast tray—hung from a similar holder. And that's all there was. No All-Jock scrubbing lotion. No Explorer's moisturizer. No Big Butch hair spray. High on my list of reasons why I loved Ben was his medicine chest. But I'd never tell him.

What with showering, examining my pores in his shaving mirror, and contemplating Ben's meager kit of supplies, stripping his bed and remaking it with fresh linen, and writing him a warm and loving note and leaving it in his typewriter so that he would miss me like the very devil when he got home, it was early afternoon before I got home myself. I knew Toni was in even before I put my key in the lock. I could hear Joan Sutherland's "Lucia" going gloriously mad in the living room.

"I thought you were going out with Ned," I said.

"I did. I'm back."

"Why so early?"

"I've hardly seen you all week. I just wanted to be here when you got back, that's all. How's Ben?"

"Fine."

"Have a good time?"

"Hmm."

"I saved the crossword for you."

I didn't have the heart to tell her Ben and I had already done it. "Thanks, but you do it. I've brought home a ton of manuscripts."

Toni curled up on the sofa with the puzzle. I flopped into a chair with a script in my lap.

"Did Pomfret drop in on you for a little chat Friday?" said Toni.

"Did he see you, too? He must be talking to all senior staff."

"He said we're not supposed to talk about what's going on."

"I know. So what do you think?"

"It's like we're being haunted, isn't it? Haunted by some kind of malevolent spirit. Like Marley's ghost. What does Ben say?"

"He won't talk about it. The only thing he'll say is that Pomfret's 'taken steps,' whatever that's supposed to mean."

"At first I really did think it was all a joke, or odd coincidences, but now I think it's more than a little scary."

"So do I." Toni scowled at her puzzle. I started on my manuscript, and the afternoon wound its slow companionable way toward evening.

Ben

ROSS SAID, "C'MON BEN, you're not eating. How come you're not eating? You didn't eat last Sunday, either. Too much loving take your appetite away?"

"Lay off, I had some breakfast with Liz before I left."

"You're supposed to have breakfast with me on Sunday. What is this? We've been doing this for years. Is she trying to fill you up so you'll lose interest?"

"Liz didn't make breakfast," I said. "I always make her breakfast on Sundays. It's a routine we have. It's nice."

"Yeah," said Ross, wistfully. "I only wish I didn't remember what it was like to spend Sunday morning in bed with a loving woman. I've been getting up at six and jogging in the park—just to have something to do, you know?"

"Yeah, I know."

"I suppose the two of you snuggle up after breakfast and do the crossword. Don't try to deny it, I can see it in your eyes, Beniamino. You have the eyes of a man who has contentment with his woman, as Hemingway would say."

I nibbled on some nachos and washed them down with beer.

"Or, do I detect a tiny snake in your Eden? Tell Uncle Ross. Is she spending all her time primping? Does she tease you all day long and then refuse to put out? Has she started getting moody and bitchy yet? You're shaking your head. You take it from your Uncle Ross, Beniamino. She may not be doing these things now, but she will."

"She doesn't do any of those things. But I'll tell you one thing, Ross—loving a woman who has a best friend as close as Toni is, is worse then having a mother-in-law. There's a connection between them that I can't even begin to tap into. In a weird way they're like Siamese twins. Siamese twins with ESP. Sometimes, I think they communicate with each other by as yet undiscovered brain waves. I told her once I was mystified by the way they defer to each other all the time. 'You're not even sisters,' I said, and Liz said, 'Toni's better than a sister. You can't choose your sister.'"

"Don't get me started on her friend Toni. She's what my father used to call a 'ghastly woman.'"

"She's not that bad. When you get to know her. It's too bad you two didn't hit it off."

"If you're looking for someone to get her off your back, you've come to the wrong guy. Besides, if we had hit it off we'd be hanging out with you two all the time, and I don't think I could take it. For someone who used to be a hard-nosed guy, you're giving a damned good imitation of an old-fashioned lovesick swain."

Ross was right. Lovesick was pretty much how I felt about Liz. I loved every inch of her sweetly beautiful body. I loved the way she was sophisticated without being snobbish and pretentious. She had a no-nonsense forthrightness, a frankness I'd never met in a woman before. Liz took me as I was, warts and all, and she expected me to do the same with her. She didn't hide behind a pink smoke screen pretending to be some kind of superior being. She was a woman who said, 'This is what I am. If you want me, you must take me as I am.' The way I look at it, that's a great compliment to pay a man. And that's how I wanted her, exactly as she was.

We had lain in bed for hours and told each other all kinds of things. I'd never opened up so much to a woman, or a man, when it comes to that, as I had to Liz. I'd told her more about myself than I realized I even knew. Some nights we fell asleep talking—murmuring, really—tales of our lives braiding together like our breaths. I loved to hold her in my arms and listen, her lips moving against my throat, my hand on her breast. One night she told me how, when they were fourteen, she and her best friend, Bunny, practiced kissing, because they weren't really sure how to do it, and they wanted to be prepared in case they got dates for the eighth-grade Halloween party. I could see them so clearly—two gangling girls, all knees, with the sweet awkwardness of colts, trying to figure out where the noses go. Where the tongues go. I loved her for telling me that.

"Ross," I said. "I think I'm really in love this time."

"It's time for you to get away, old buddy. It's time for you to get a little perspective on this before things get out of hand and you do something you're sure to re-

gret. How about going fishing with me next month?
The Press will be practically shut down. There's never
anyone left in Publishers' Row during August. What do
you say we fly to Michigan and rent a car and drive over
to the Big Two-Hearted River and do a little fly-fishing.
I don't mean the one in the Upper Peninsula, I mean old
Hemingway's real stomping ground, the Fox. This
would be a great time. You know we've been talking
about it for years. Now's the time. Let's do it. Whad-
daya say?"

"I don't know. I'll have to think about it."

"Okay. If you don't want to go west, we could go
bonefishing in Key West."

"Give me a chance to think about it, Ross."

"You'll think about it?"

"I'll think about it."

Liz

BY THE TIME EVENING CAME, I'd burrowed my way into
the middle of a manuscript only to realize I'd read the
same paragraph three times. Obviously my mind was
somewhere else. I kept wondering why I had so little
difficulty putting my finger on the problems in a book,
but I couldn't seem to apply the same acumen to my
own life. Was it only a matter of critical distance?

Toni opened a bottle of wine, and I cut hard-boiled
eggs into wedges for a "Salade niçoise."

"We're into July already," I said. "I can hardly believe it."

"Tell me about it," said Toni, washing romaine in the
sink. "Production promised me they'd bird-dog that
tricky cover..."

"*Love's Labors?*"

"That's the one. Someone over there must have been asleep at the switch, so it's back to square one, and the press date is Tuesday. You know where we'll be if we lose our press date—we'll be lucky to print before Christmas." She cranked the salad spinner so violently it rumbled ominously, threatening to self-destruct.

I knew better than to say, *Stop worrying, it's not your problem, it's production's problem.* Toni was born worrying. Her department executed the book jacket, ergo, she'd fret over it until she saw it safely in the bookstore windows.

I waited until I'd finished topping and tailing the beans before I said, "In a couple of weeks you can forget about all that. In a couple of weeks we go to Avignon."

"And not a minute too soon. For four blessed weeks I'm going to do absolutely nothing but lie in the sun. And swim. Remember that darling guy who came last summer to clean the pool? Joel? I wonder if they still have Joel . . . ?"

"Are you sure you don't want to ask Ned?"

"Why are you harping on Ned? I told you months ago he couldn't make it, even if I did want him there, which I don't. I've been looking forward to the two of us having the place to ourselves, just like we've always done." She looked up suddenly, catching what I suppose must have been guilt written all over my face. "You don't want to go away for a month and leave Ben. That's what you've been working up to, isn't it?"

"Well . . ."

"Have you asked him?"

"No, I haven't asked him. I wouldn't ask him without talking it over with you, you know that."

"Do I?"

"Don't be a silly ass. Of course you do. I do love him, Toni. I don't think I could bear the thought of a whole month away from him."

"Then you'd better ask him."

"You don't mind? You're sure you don't mind?"

"Have you considered what you'll do if he says no?"

I not only hadn't considered it—it had never so much as crossed my mind. "Stay here in New York?"

"Then I sure hope you can persuade him, because I don't want to spend *my* vacation in New York."

"But why would you stay here, just because I didn't go?"

Toni clamped the can opener on the tuna can with so much force a geyser of oil spurted across the table. She cranked as she spoke. "Avignon...is something we do...together.... We've always...done it...together.... It wouldn't be any good...alone."

I CALLED BEN later that night. "How was your breakfast with Ross?"

"Okay. Did you get a lot of work done?"

"Quite a bit, but not so much as I'd hoped. What did you do?"

"We went to a movie."

"Any good?"

"It was one of those French films by someone named Luc or Claude. I couldn't keep my mind on the subtitles. My attention kept wandering to other things."

"Such as?"

"Fishing, mostly."

I couldn't very well expect him to think of me every waking moment. But fishing? "The French are crazy about fishing—they'll toss a line into a puddle after a heavy rain."

"Yeah? Never been there. Don't speak the language."

This was my opening, a heaven-sent opportunity to bring up the subject of vacationing together. In France. But I didn't bring it up. I could hear my voice in my head saying, *We'll have such a marvelous time, darling—just the three of us, you and me and Toni.* Like Scarlett O'Hara I decided to think about it tomorrow.

12

I WAS SITTING on my office floor with the better part of
a chapter fanned out around me. Sometimes, seeing all
the scenes in one take will help me to see where something has gone wrong with the story's flow. It's hard to
explain, but I was trying to pass through the book to
see it from the other side, and just when I thought I'd
put my finger on the problem, the phone rang. I reached
up to my desk and felt for the receiver without taking
my eyes from the pages.

"Liz?" said a voice I failed to recognize, so deep was
my concentration. "This is Ned. I've got to talk to you."

"Oh," I finally managed, after what I knew was too
long a pause. "Ned! Toni's Ned."

"Actually, that's what I want to talk to you about. I'm
at the bar around the corner from the Press. I need your
help, Liz. Toni's going to need your help. I've got to talk
to you."

I glanced at my watch. It was just four o'clock; I
wasn't meeting with Mr. Pomfret until five. "What is
this all about?"

"I can't talk about it over the phone. Please, Liz."

I looked at the pages all around me, and I sighed. "I'll
be there in five minutes," I said reluctantly. Ned had an
actor's talent for self-dramatization.

"A favor," he said, just as I was about to hang up.
"Don't say anything to Toni."

Why was he being so mysterious? It couldn't have anything to do with his soap opera—he never confided anything to me about his work. Perhaps he was planning some sort of surprise for Toni, something he needed my help to set up. But what? It couldn't be her birthday, because that had been in March: Ned gave her a cardigan from L. L. Bean. Whatever nice thing he had in mind for her, it was about time, as far as I was concerned. I'd never much cared for Ned. I didn't like the cavalier way he treated Toni, but I'd always kept my own counsel and stayed out of it, because as long as we'd known each other, Toni and I had an unspoken compact between us: we did not criticize each other's choice of men. Not much, anyway. For the almost five years that Toni had known Ned, I'd done my best to keep my opinions to myself. Strictly closemouthed and nonjudgmental, that was me. But when push came to shove, the plain, unvarnished truth was that I thought he was a perfect twit. Naturally, I'd never ever said so.

When they first started going out together, I used to wonder what it was, exactly, that Toni got out of it. Anyone would.

"I can see what you call his Caravaggio profile," I'd say, and then wait for her to fill in all the blank spots. But Toni would go all silly and smiling. She'd coo, "Oh, Ned is soooo wonderful!" which explained nothing at all.

He was no more than a passable television actor, and one of the shallowest men I've ever met. It was Toni's misfortune that he was so extraordinarily good-looking, because that was always her downfall. His hair was like spun gold, his eyes were hazel, and his basic expression was an engagingly earnest boyishness. In the last year or so she'd sometimes been deprecating about his vanity and his self-absorption, but then she'd turn around and talk for hours about how thrilling it was to wake up and see his perfect profile on the other pillow. As for what he saw in Toni, that was all too painfully obvious—at least it was to me. Where else could he have found such unfailing devotion and admiration? Toni was more than his perfect audience, she was his greatest fan.

IT WASN'T HARD to spot Ned in the dimly lit bar. His hair glowed like a golden doubloon. He was perched at the bar—a petulant Adonis. "They're killing me off," he said as I sat down beside him. Rather than meet my eyes, he glowered into the drink on the bar in front of him.

"Do you mean Dr. Jack Jilson, alcoholic hematologist, is going down the tubes?"

"Yup."

"How can they do that? Who'll run the tests on that woman with the mysterious bumps?" Toni always kept me up to date on his character's story line. "When did you find this out?"

"They're going to run my car off a dock in Connecticut. In Bridgeport. We shot my last scene this morning, finished it before the lunch break. And they didn't even tell me until it was over. Can you believe it? They were afraid I might telegraph something. This isn't Chekhov, I told them. And all this time I thought my character was going to get promoted. I thought I'd make chief of service. Maybe assistant administrator of the hospital."

"That's terrible."

"He's always had a better wardrobe, the assistant administrator."

"That's just awful."

"His suits and shirts come from Barney's."

"I mean it's awful that they're killing you off. I'm sorry, Ned. I really am." I don't think he heard a word I said.

"There is a...um...silver lining. It's an ill wind, and all that sort of thing." He revolved his glass in careful circles on the bar. He did it beautifully, his tapered fingers touching just the rim. A very photogenic gesture.

"Silver lining?"

"The thing is...Dorrie's going out to the Coast to do a pilot for next season." Dorrie is Doris Dockweiller, the executive producer on Ned's show, of whom Toni harbored nothing but the darkest suspicions. "She's asked me to go with her...to the Coast."

"Has she really?"

"There's a great part for me..."

"I'll bet you were surprised. What is it, Judas?"

"...I play a prison psychiatrist, but it's not an ordinary prison. This is one of those cushy federal pens where they send the crooked bankers and the inside traders and the junk bond dealers, guys like that. They're always trying to get out. It's sort of an update on the old *Stalag 17*. Full of laughs. The pilot's practically presold. So it means a guaranteed thirteen weeks."

"Why are you telling me this? Why aren't you telling Toni?"

He gulped a manly slug of his drink and turned to face me. His eyes looked like ice cubes. "I'm going to tell her. I'm going to tell her." He said it twice. The perfect picture of a man screwing up his resolve with eighty-proof Dutch courage. "She's meeting me here at five-thirty. It's just that I wanted you to know first, because you know how much she . . . you know how infatuated with me . . ." He positively preened as he said it.

"She loves you."

" . . . and this is going to hit her awfully hard. Awfully hard. She's going to need your help."

"Are you telling me you're not coming back? You're breaking off with Toni?"

"The thing is, Liz . . ." He jacked himself up with another slug. "I think I've outgrown her."

"You've outgrown *her*? Ned, you really are the world's biggest horse's ass."

I MADE IT BACK to the Press in seven minutes flat, but Toni wasn't in her office. Her secretary said she'd left for an appointment an hour ago and wasn't expected back until tomorrow. Yes, said the secretary, Toni had taken a call from Ned before she left.

At least Ben was in. He was staring glumly at a set of galleys, the margins a maze of author's alterations and untimely additions.

"Welcome to never-never land," he said. "The country where books are never finished because authors never, never quit re-writing."

"Darling, I'm sorry to break in like this . . ."

"It's a blessing. You've brightened my day beyond measure. Come kiss me quick. It'll give me strength."

I did exactly that, and it was lovely. "Darling, I have to rush, but I had to stop and tell you I can't have dinner with you tonight."

"Of course you can. I've already made a reservation at that new Brazilian place on Seventy-second Street."

"Not tonight. I have to be home for Toni. Ned's running out on her, the little fink. He's going out to the Coast. I've got to run, I'm late for a meeting with Pomfret."

Poor Mr. Pomfret. I flew into his office, chattered at him like a crazed cockatoo, finishing my presentation in exactly twenty-six minutes, thirty-seven seconds, thus winning the fast-talkers' traveling trophy, hurled myself down the stairs and fled back to the bar. Toni was not there, neither was Ned.

I waved the bartender over. "That blond man I was talking to about an hour ago—did a woman meet him here at around five-thirty?"

"Curly red hair?" he said. "About so high?" He held out his hand at midchest.

"That's the one."

"Honey, you shudda been here. She really pasted him a good one."

"Pasted him? Toni? She couldn't have. She can't even kill a spider."

"Listen," he said, resting his forearms on the bar between us. "In my line of work you see all kinds. Now this lady was a lady who was bitched, pardon my French. You can take it from me who's seen a few. That guy she decked is going to have the biggest, blackest black eye since Kid Chance went fifteen rounds with Marcel Cerdan. It was just like that song. "Frankie and Johnny." She did her man in, 'cause he done her wrong. *Whammo!* Know what I mean? And she walked out of here with her head high. She walked out of here like a queen."

She may have held her head up, but I knew she had to be in purgatory. "Where's your phone?" I said. The apartment phone rang three times and then the answering machine picked up. I waited impatiently for the beep.

"Toni, it's Liz. Pick up if you're there. I know about Ned. Pick up so we can talk. Toni? Talk to me, Toni." But she didn't pick up. She wouldn't talk, not even to me. I knew she was there. I don't know how I knew, but I knew. I went out on the street and tried to flag a cab.

I FOUND TONI slumped on the living-room sofa staring at an untouched glass of red wine, her mouth so compressed I couldn't see her lips. Her eyes were red and puffy in a face as white as dough. There was a box of tissues at her feet. The floor was littered with pink wads.

"Toni! Oh, Toni. I got here as soon as I could." I sat down beside her and put my arms around her.

"What am I going to do?" she asked, gripping me hard. "What am I going to do?" Her face crumpled and she buried it in my shoulder, her body racked with sobs.

I hugged her to me, patting her back, smoothing her hair. We rocked back and forth like mourners at a wake. I muttered, "Go ahead, get it all out, it'll do you good." And in the next breath, "Don't cry, darling, he's not worth one drop of your tears." I murmured anything comforting that came into my head. Logic had no place here.

Toni wept and wept, first violently, then with a relentless steady rhythm of deep, gulping breaths and shuddering sobs. Even her legs were trembling. And my own tears mingled with hers at the sight of her in so much pain. Her face was so hot against my cheek.

Slowly, hiccuping, she subsided. We both grabbed handfuls of tissue and blew our noses. "Oh, Liz," she said, catching her lower lip between her teeth. "He was so beautiful. And his skin has no grain. Did I ever tell you that? No grain—he has skin like a Flemish portrait."

"He lied to you," I said, wiping my eyes.

"I know."

"How can you care about his skin when he's been sleeping with Dorrie. You've suspected that for a long time—you told me so yourself."

"I know. But that doesn't make it any easier. I always thought that somehow that business with Dorrie would blow over. What has she got that I don't have?"

"She's a producer, you goose. She's got jobs. And as far as Ned is concerned, that means she's got him by the short-hairs. Loyalty is a virtue that that man knows nothing about."

"Have you ever seen her? She must be fifteen years older than Ned." She leaned back and closed her eyes, and the tears seeped down her cheeks in glittering runnels.

"Oh, Toni, don't," I pleaded. "He's not worth it. You're worth ten thousand Neds. I can't stand seeing you tear yourself up like this over such a . . . such a . . ." Everything I'd kept bottled up about Ned threatened to come tumbling out. I clamped my jaws shut, shaking with rage at Ned for hurting her so. Was I wrong, all these years, in not telling her how much I disliked the man? Could I have prevented this? Was it my duty to tell her? Surely, some of the blame must be mine.

"My hand hurts," she said, her voice as soft and breathy as an injured child. She held out her right hand for me to examine. The first three knuckles were scraped raw. A purple bruise was spreading across the back and down the fingers.

"The bartender told me you hit him. 'Decked him' was the way he put it. He was very impressed with you. He said Ned's going to have a dilly of a black eye."

"I don't know what came over me. I've never hit anyone in my life before. 'Decked him?' Is that was he said?" She giggled and licked tears from her upper lip. "Ned looked so surprised. I know I shouldn't have done it, but—"

"If anyone ever had justifiable cause, you did. Can you move your fingers? Do you think your hand is broken? Go ahead, let me see you move your fingers."

Wincing, she waggled her fingers. "They all work, but it hurts like hell."

"Let me get you some ice." I was relieved to have something concrete to do. In the kitchen I threw ice cube trays into the sink with a tremendously satisfying crash, then worked off some of my anger and frustration by smashing the cubes with a meat mallet. I filled a plastic bag with ice and bound it gently to the back of Toni's hand by wrapping a tea towel around it.

Toni gulped back a sob. "I don't know what I'd do without you."

"Well, you don't have to worry about that, because you'll never have to do without me. And I certainly don't plan on ever doing without you. We've made something of a habit of binding up each other's wounds, haven't we?"

Toni sniffed. "A lot of years of tender loving care, babe."

"Remember the time I had two wisdom teeth pulled at once and they both turned into dry-sockets? You were the only thing that kept me from going right out the window. Remember that? You stayed with me for a week feeding me painkillers and sherbet and keeping me away from the window."

"God, you looked awful. You lost six pounds and looked like the Wicked Witch of the West with the world's biggest hangover."

"You never told me that," I protested. "You said I looked just like Jennifer Jones in the last reel of *The Son of Bernadette.*"

"I lied. The year after that we sweated out my biopsy and your D and C. Oh, Lord, but we've gotten each other over a lot of humps, haven't we?"

We hugged, in confirmation, needing no words. Finally, I said, "Why don't you have a shower, and I'll make something to eat."

"I'm not hungry."

"Soup? A little bit of soup. You can always eat soup."

"Cream of tomato?"

"Cream of tomato." This was Toni's soul-food. As a cook she knew her way around the cuisines of six different countries, but when she was unhappy, or in pain, canned tomato soup was her consolation. It had to be canned. She liked to break saltines into it. It was pure comfort food and always soothed her troubled soul.

Steam rose from the saucepan, pungent, sharp—I'd sneaked in a bay leaf. Toni wandered into the kitchen, her face shining and her hair damp. She wore a thick white terry cloth robe that reached the floor. The bag of ice was wrapped around her hand again. She looked a shade less disconsolate. I poured the soup into a bowl and set it at her place beside a plate of crackers. She stared into the bowl, blinking, as though not sure what it contained.

"Eat," I insisted. "It'll do you good."

Awkwardly, she took up the spoon in her left hand, dipped it clumsily into the soup and craning her neck like a hungry chick, sipped. "It's good," she said, setting down the spoon to crumble crackers into the bowl. "Thanks. What are you having?"

"I'll nibble on the left-over chicken. How about you? Do you want some?"

She shook her head, and more skillfully now, skimmed a piece of soup-swollen cracker from the surface of her soup.

I put down my chicken leg. "I know it won't be easy, but if you can just get through the next couple of weeks, we'll be out of here. We'll be in Avignon, and we can have the whole month to ourselves. No pressures. No men. Just us."

"I thought you were going to ask Ben. I thought you'd already asked him."

"Well, I haven't."

"I'm glad. It'll be just the two of us. Just like it's always been."

"Yes, just like it's always been."

After a few more mouthfuls, she looked up over her spoon, her eyes startled. "How could I have been so blind? How could I have been such a fool over Ned?"

"Show me a woman who has never been a fool over some man—" I waved my chicken leg in the air "—and I'll show you a nun."

Toni giggled and the soup in her spoon spilled back into the bowl. Two large tears slid down her cheeks toward her mouth. She sniffed and licked them away. "The hell of it is, if he came through the door right this minute and said it was all a mistake, I'd take him back."

"Toni! You wouldn't!"

"No, no I wouldn't. But you know, he has the most beautiful hands..."

An hour later Toni was tucked up in bed, her poor bruised hand resting on the bedspread, her face a pale squinched thing on the pillow, a crumpled nasturtium.

"BUT YOU CAN'T GO," said Ben. We were in his office the following morning, drinking coffee. I had just told him about Ned and how I hoped our annual trek to Provence would help Toni write finis to his dreadful chapter in her life. "That's why I have to go," I concluded.

"Not now," he said adamantly, his mouth a stubborn line and his big square jaw looking as hard as granite. "You can't go."

"What do you mean, I can't go? Why ever not?"

"What about us? How can you take off and leave me stranded like a gasping trout?"

"Somehow I can't see you as a gasping trout."

"Liz...darling...I need you."

That made my heart beat faster. "Darling!" was the best I could manage.

"I don't know how it's happened, but you're a part of my life..."

"And you of mine, but—"

"...a part of me, almost. Besides, you know I can't go two days without making love to you. How could I last a whole month? Liz, baby, I'll go crazy. You'll go crazy."

He had me there. "I never said it would be easy, Ben, I'll want you every minute I'm away, you know that. I want you all the time, as it is. There's nothing in the world I'd rather do at this very moment that wrap myself around you and sink into a great big double bed, but . . ."

"Liz—"

"There are times when women have to be alone. This is one of those times."

"But what about us?" he said again.

"Ben, darling," I said, touching his cheek. "You have to understand that I have more than one 'us' in my life. Toni and I are an 'us,' too. And she needs me right now because she's hurting. I have to do what I can to help her through the pain, and if that means we go off to France alone for a month, well, that's something you and I will just have to accept. Toni and I are buddies, like you and Ross. I can't let her down."

He kissed me then and shook his head. "No, you're not like me and Ross. We're buddies, you two are a team. You're really a doubles act."

It didn't, of course, end there. Ben and I talked about little else for the next couple of weeks. We talked about it in bed, and we talked about it at the office. We talked about it the last thing before falling asleep and the first thing in the morning. Maybe not absolutely the very first thing. But right afterward.

"What it comes down to," I explained one morning in the shower, "is that at this precise moment, Toni is very down on men. Bend your head so I can shampoo your hair. And who can blame her?"

"Hmm," he muttered, his chin tucked into his breastbone. "Harder."

"If I rub any harder you'll have ridges in your skull."

"Feels good."

"Keep your eyes closed. As I said, she's very anti-men right now."

"But I'm not the personification of Man. I'm me. Why should she see me as a symbol. Do I look like a symbol? Do I look like a threat? It doesn't make sense. I'm just me, good ol' Ben. Trusty ol' Ben. Loving ol' Ben. Ooow, that feels good."

"Don't try to make yourself sound like Old Badger, it doesn't fit." I slithered my soapy hands over his chest. "You may be furry, darling, but you're not that furry."

"Surely Toni is capable of drawing a distinction between me and Men."

"'Hell hath no fury...' Now rinse."

"I'm not the one who scorned her. It has nothing to do with me. I want to be with you, Liz."

He didn't have to tell me that, I could see it, and what I felt at the sight of him was very close to raw power. It's intoxicating to know that I have only to touch Ben, and he will grow before my eyes into this powerful, stalked being, shaped for our perfect mutual gratification. It's an amazing feeling. And as we stood there with the water pouring over us, both of us looking down, watching him become this wondrous other being, this pleasuring creature, I knew I'd never be able to find the strength to be separated from him for a whole month. How could I think of going to France without him? Four long weeks without him. Thirty-one nights of emptiness. Just thinking about it made me ache. It felt like the fraying rope in a tug-of-war.

TONI AND I MET TWICE at the Press that day. Once in her office and once in mine, but I waited until we got home that night before I said anything. This was not the sort of thing to talk about at work. We stopped on the way home and bought some smoked turkey, a sweet red pepper and a bulb of fennel, and a wedge of runny Camembert. Toni put on a new recording of *The Barber of Seville*. I took this as a sign that her spirits were on the rise.

We'd worked our way through several difficult, though no doubt therapeutic, weeks of the last act of Mozart's *Don Giovanni*. Other times we had snatches of Carmen telling Don José to go to hell—he wasn't going to tell *her* what to do. But tonight, wonder of wonders, we had left all the carnage behind and moved to sunny, tune-filled Seville. Some of it even made Toni giggle, just as it used to. I waited until we were settled in the living room with our coffee.

"Would you mind," I said finally, "that is, under the circumstances, would it make you terribly uncomfortable if I did ask Ben to join us in Avignon? Just for the last two weeks?"

She looked up from her coffee, her face a mask. "I thought you'd given up on that idea."

"It's not as though you and I won't be together, because we will. We'll have two weeks to ourselves, and after that it'll still be just like it's always been, except that Ben will be there, too."

"Exactly the same only different?"

"Toni, please, don't be like that."

"Like what?"

"He wants so much to go."

"Then you did ask him."

"I didn't. It was his idea. I love him, Toni. I really do. I don't know how to say no to him when he's so adamant about wanting to be with me."

"You want him there just as much as he wants to be there, don't you?"

"Yes."

"Then I think you'd better ask him, and make it official. There's no point in having *both* of us wandering around unhinged by love like a crazy opera heroine...."

13

Ben

"DON'T GO," said Ross. "Those two women will eat you alive."

"Ahh! You don't know anything about them."

"I've seen enough of them to know the type, Beniamino. They'll cut you up in dainty little pieces and have you for lunch on toast."

I couldn't explain it to Ross. I couldn't tell him I was afraid that if Liz and I were separated now—when we'd become so close, closer than I'd ever been with anyone—some terribly essential link, some tie I couldn't define would be broken, and I would lose her. We would lose each other—the ocean between us would see to that.

"Are you afraid she'll find solace with some Frenchman?"

"She'd never do that."

"Never say never where women are concerned. 'I'll never lie to you,' they say. 'Our love will never die,' they say. 'I'll never leave you,' they say. Forget it, Ben. Give it a rest. She'll be that much hungrier for you when she comes back. Forget Provence. Let's go fishing. Let's go get us some trout."

"I have to go, Ross. It's something I have to do."

"Little tiny pieces, buddy. You just think of me dapping flies on a cold clear stream while they're prancing around making mincemeat out of you."

As IT TURNED OUT, I didn't go to France with them. Liz convinced me it would be better all around if they had some time alone to settle in before I arrived. I could see that adding to their anxieties wouldn't win me any points.

"Go ahead," I said to Liz. "I'm not so blind I can't see that it'll do Toni good to be alone with you."

"Are you sure?"

"You just have a good time. I'll see you in a couple of weeks." I thought I was being understanding and unselfish, if not downright noble. I wonder now if in my heart of hearts I didn't have some premonition of what would happen.

Somehow, I managed to make it through two of the longest weeks of my life. Fourteen nights without making love to Liz. Fourteen mornings without waking up with Liz in my arms. I started going to the gym again—working out after work helped me sleep, and I got through a lot of work at the Press.

With everyone on vacation, there was no one at the Press but Mr. Pomfret and me. The two of us put our heads together and spent a day speculating about the plague of misfortunes that had befallen the Press. We looked at every occurrence, examined every angle. Then we drew up a plan.

I called Liz that afternoon to tell her I'd booked a flight, but it was one of those crackly echoing connections where every word crosses the Atlantic trailed by its echo. It was impossible to decode her emotional weather when all I could make out was something like, "...do love you, love you...but better, better to wait, wait."

"I love you too much to wait. I'll be there tomorrow. Liz? Liz? Are you there?" But all I could hear was a rush of air and a faint voice saying, " . . . too, too."

I was still staring at the phone when Pomfret put his head in my office. "Are you sure this holiday of yours won't interfere with...hmm, what we've been discussing?"

"You have my number," I assured him. With a little bit of luck he'd never have to use it.

By THE TIME I ARRIVED in Avignon, I was so tired I thought I was walking in my sleep. The night before, Ross had organized a farewell evening at Shea Stadium where we watched the Cubs clobber the Mets. After a defeat like that, there was nothing to do but repair to Doyle's where we could share our disappointment with some other diehard fans, and, incidentally, hoist a couple of farewell noggins.

I think I had about six minutes sleep. The next morning, with Ross's parting words still buzzing in my ears—"Remember what I said, pal. Don't let them chop you up"—I left for France. I felt a little self-conscious wearing sunglasses against the glare, but it was that or instant brain damage. My recollection of my arrival is somewhat vague, as I try to recall it. It was late afternoon, early evening by the time I landed in Paris and hopped a fast train down to Provence. It was dark when I finally made it to Avignon exhausted and gritty, my eyes gummy and my ears humming.

Liz was waiting on the platform, a cool tower of blond perfection in a white linen dress. *Where's Toni?* I wondered as I walked toward her. Then I took her in my arms and lost myself in her kiss. Her body was so sweetly familiar pressing against mine that I must have missed the signals she was sending out.

"I've missed you," I said, my mouth still against hers.

"Oh, Ben," she said, pulling away, "I've missed you, too, you must know that. But why have you come? I mean, why now? I didn't expect you for another ten days."

"Isn't that obvious? To be with you."

"But I need to be with Toni just now. Things have finally begun to really smooth out, if you know what I mean."

"Now you can be with both of us."

She stared at me hard, the whiteness of her dress dazzling in the harsh platform lights. "You don't understand. She needs my support."

"So do I, Liz. So do I."

Toni was waiting at the car. She grinned and gave me a peck on the cheek. She looked better than she had in New York—rested, tanned, relaxed. She looked in control, for a change. "You must be bushed," she said. "We'll have you home in no time."

Toni drove. Liz and I sat in the back separated by resentment and longing. Neither of us looked at the other. I remember pulling up to an elaborate wrought iron gate set in a high stone wall and Toni hopping out with a giant key in her hands to open it. The halves of the gate creaked as they swung back. Tires crunched across a graveled yard. In the headlights I could see a low, stuccoed house, pale yellow ocher walls, a red-tiled roof, windows covered by heavy brown shutters. It was very plain, with tubs of flowers beside big double doors of what looked like age-blackened oak. Toni dug another dungeon-sized key out of her shoulder bag and unlocked the front doors.

"This way," said Liz, kicking off her sandals. I followed her pink heels up the stairs, lugging my bag. Her room—our room—was crammed with dressers and chairs, two wardrobes, a pier glass, and the most inviting double bed in all of Europe.

I looked from the bed to Liz, but it was as though some vital communication link between us had been short-circuited. She crossed purposefully to the window, pushed open the shutters and headed for the door. "Come down and have some coffee or a glass of wine or something to eat—it'll help you sleep." So cool in her white dress, so contained, so self-sufficient. At that moment I wanted her to need me as much as I needed her.

"Your loving is the only thing I need to help me sleep." She smiled as she turned away, but her gaze was unfocused and her shoulders tense. She shrugged in a way that reminded me of Toni. Were they turning into each other, I wondered, melding into identical twins?

I found a bathroom and splashed cold water on my face and combed my hair with my fingers. I was so tired I had a hard time focusing on my face in the mirror. Should I shave? Just in case? To hell with it, I thought. But at the head of the stairs I turned back, got my kit and shaved. Hope springs eternal.

Liz and Toni bustled around the kitchen table setting out bowls of olives, black, iridescent, and packages of cheese. A sausage appeared. A plate of figs. Liz poured water into a high-tech coffee machine. Toni opened a bottle of wine. I walked into the kitchen convinced I'd somehow stumbled onto a stage in the middle of a play, one that had started a long, long time before I came in.

I drank a glass of wine and ate some cheese. After the second glass of wine I could feel my head bobbing.

"Go up and get some sleep," said Liz.

"You look like you're ready to fall over," said Toni.

"Aren't you coming up?" I said to Liz, blinking.

"I'll be up later," she said. "There's a movie on TV we want to watch and then—"

"We always have a swim before we turn in," said Toni, finishing Liz's thought.

I fell into the double bed and slept like the dead.

I wakened to the faint creak of the opening door. I lay on my side, watching through slitted eyes as Liz tiptoed into the room. Her dress glittered blue-white in the moonlight streaming through the window. Her mouth was darkly vivid, her eyes shadowed. She glanced at me as she unbuttoned the front of her dress. I feigned sleep. I had always loved watching her undress—the oh, so casual, almost negligent way she revealed her treasures always excited me. But in that room, beneath the caressing moon, in the warm, scented night, there was about her a voluptuous languor I had never seen before, and I found it almost unbearably erotic. She stepped out of her dress. Instantly my blood started pounding, cannons of desire boomed through me. She reached behind her back in that amazing way women do and opened her bra. Her breasts pointed up to the top of the mirror, and the blood pounded in my throat. In one smooth motion, she stepped out of her panties to pose, one hand in her hair, the other on her hip, studying her profile in the moon-bright mirror. My mouth went dry.

I sat up in bed and held my face to her as though she were the sun. She came toward me gravely, her breasts trembling with each step. The skin around my eyes felt tight, my legs trembled with desire.

"I'm sorry, I didn't mean to wake you. I just came up for my robe. We're going to swim."

"Come here." My voice sounded harsh, my throat was so tight with longing.

"But Toni's waiting—"

That was as far as she got. I took her hands and pulled her down onto the bed beside me, covering her mouth with kisses, luring her clever, elusive tongue, taming it. Panting, breathless, we came up for air.

"You taste like a moon goddess," I whispered, my tongue still lingering at her lips.

"And how does a moon goddess taste?" The tip of her tongue teased mine.

"Of wine and sweet figs, the thick, dark honey of love."

"If I am a goddess, then you are Pan, my darkling creature of the forest." With strong hands she stroked my thighs, sighing deeply. "I shouldn't be here. I'm supposed to be down at the pool."

"Just one more kiss," I pleaded. "One more and I'll let you go."

"One more," she agreed, but that kiss had no ending, and the passion of her kisses was a goddess's passion—wild and ecstatic. We buried ourselves in love's receiving flesh, rolling over and over, clinging to each other like shipwrecked sailors on a sea of love, left gasping by waves of wracking desire.

With tongue and kisses I traced the curve of her delicate ears, followed the line of her throat to the sweet hollow at the base where I hid a hundred kisses. I captured her trembling breasts, held them in the hollow of my hand, whispered ancient Pan-tales to them, tales told in a tongue only they could understand. They swelled at my mouth's cajoling, while Liz, gripping my shoulders as though she were clinging to a rock ledge, moaned softly beneath me, her hips moving sinuously against the hot and urgent hardness of my desire. The air was perfumed, hot and thick and we sweated in our eagerness, our bodies sliding against each other, oiled by love.

I raised myself above her, supporting myself on my elbows. Her hips followed me hungrily. "Now are you glad I came?"

"I didn't know," she said, panting, "that I could miss anyone as much as I've missed you, want anyone as much as I want you."

I took her then. Took her as the great god Pan took the nymphs of the woods—with a single stroke piercing to the root of her pulsing desire—and the air whistled in her throat like a bird cry, and it growled in her chest like a tigress as she urged me again and again and yet again into the white-hot glistening core of her where we exploded together, love like lava pouring from us.

How long we lay, panting and exhausted on that love-soaked bed, I don't know. "Don't move," she had whispered. "Please don't move." So I stayed where I was, over her, in her. Her eyes were closed and on her moonlit face an expression of such calm, such happiness, I thought I might burst with pride, or weep with my own joy, or both at once. It was a flicker of a shadow that made me glance up.

In the mirror I saw Toni standing in the doorway, her hands balled into fists, her face a pale ghost's face, her mouth an anguished O. Her eyes met mine, and the next instant she was gone.

THE BIRDS WOKE ME. They called and whistled and twittered; I didn't recognize a single birdcall. They were French birds singing their own songs. How strange it was to wake to the calls of birds who sang in French.

Liz was asleep. She lay on her back, her pale blue nightie concealing nothing. I wanted to make love again, but I hadn't the heart to wake her. It was hot. Sweat was already trickling down my chest. A hot wind lifted a tiny blue ribbon threaded through the top of her nightie. For half a second I thought of taking her in her sleep, then rejected the idea. I left her alone in her sleep.

The hot wind sighed through the half-open shutters. From the window I saw the backyards of half a dozen houses, gardens, pools. The pool beneath our window sparkled blindingly blue. A high stone wall surrounded the garden, screened it from its neighbors. Palm trees cast morning shadows, but what were the other trees? I couldn't name them. Plane trees? Umbrella pines? I was guessing. I didn't know those trees. They were not American trees. I saw a row of what I thought might be cypress, a green so deep it was nearly black, tall, twisted upon themselves. The air smelled of flowers I couldn't name—foreign blooms, exotic in their anonymity.

I headed for the nearest bathroom where I showered with a gadget that looked like a telephone receiver. There was no shower curtain. It took fifteen minutes, three towels and the bath mat to sop up the floor. I felt hulking and clumsy. What am I doing here, I asked myself, an inarticulate foreigner who can barely puzzle out the simplest sign?

Liz was gone when I got back to the bedroom, the bed was made. She had propped a note against my hairbrush on the dresser: *Gone for bread, back soon. Kiss-kiss, L.* I pulled on my swimsuit and headed for the pool. I swam laps in the bright morning air, the water so warm I might have been swimming through the exotic blue ether of some distant planet. Bubbles of breath streamed from my mouth past my ears like swirling galaxies. I was hypnotized by the silver stream of bubbles, by the rhythmic movement of my arms and legs. I was a man-fish, slicing silver through the water, breathing silver breath.

My ankles were caught, trapped, and I was pulled under, down to the bottom of the blue water-world. Beneath me, skimming the bottom, Liz and Toni appeared as suddenly, as startlingly as sea nymphs. Silent water-laughter bubbled from their mouths. They released me, and our three heads broke the surface, gasping for breath, shaking the water out of our eyes, laughing.

I looked into Toni's eyes, looked for a message waiting there for me. But there was nothing. She smiled—an all-pals-together sort of smile. I smiled back, but I didn't believe it.

The sun was so hot it seared the moisture from our bodies, prickling, sharp. We were dry almost instantly.

We dressed and breakfasted on crusty bread and sweet butter, raspberry jam, and coffee with hot milk drunk from cups the size of chili bowls. The radio on the counter alternated songs I'd never heard with news I couldn't understand. We wore shorts and T-shirts and sandals. Liz had pulled on one of my shirts. I'd always found this mildly erotic, and she knew it. She and Toni had been talking about the latest scandal at the Paris Opera. Liz broke off to smile at me over the rim of her coffee cup. A languid smile, honeyed with memories and promise. She wasn't wearing a bra. Her nipple winked knowingly from behind Sausalito Baits.

Liz and Toni were composing a shopping list. They twittered, heads together. The wind rattled the shutters. The leaves of palm trees rasped high above the house. I don't know what kind of house I expected. Something fairly simple, I suppose. Perhaps, along the lines of a renovated farmhouse. But of course I didn't know what French farmhouses actually looked like, my meager knowledge of Gallic rural architecture having been drawn entirely from old Hollywood movies— brave Résistance fighter blows up Nazi train and escapes to win the heart of the baker's beautiful sloe-eyed daughter—the flickering romances of my boyhood Saturday afternoons.

This was no rustic, trapdoored kitchen with smoky hams hanging from a beamed ceiling and garlands of garlic and onions strung from the rafters. The floor was blue-gray slate, the walls white, the cabinets black plastic veined with swirls of gold. The cabinets pretended to be marble—a facetious pretense. Every electronic cooking device known to man was represented here, from a Cuisinart big enough to make hash browns for an entire army division, to a microwave oven and a conventional gas range with six burners and three ovens. *Why three?* The electric can opener looked tough enough to open a submarine. I marveled at the number and variety of these devices and wondered why the French hadn't yet discovered the shower curtain.

Liz and Toni, string bags over their arms, trotted off to shop their way down their list. I followed, the designated carrier. We drove to the farmers' market in town. Under one great roof were scores of stalls as exotic to me as a souk in Marrakech—fruit sellers, vegetable sellers, fishmongers, butchers, cheese stalls, bakers, wine sellers. Who would believe, unless they had seen this, that there could be so many different kinds of cheese or olives or ham?

I inhaled deeply the sharp iodine tang of the sea, stared back at wide-eyed fish laid on seaweed and ice. I felt less a stranger here with fish I knew—snapper, cod, rockfish, flounder, sole, sardines no bigger than smelt. The camaraderie of the sea, I suppose. I recognized black-shelled mussels, gnarled and barnacled clams, eels as thick and black as tarred hawsers, filleted anchovies that looked like purple-brown ribbons.

We breathed in the home-smell of freshly baked bread, the loamy smell of vegetables, carrots with the moist earth still clinging to them. It was hot, everyone was sweating. The air was clamorous with earnest talk of transactions and quality, with laughter and friends hailing one another, greetings called, farewells shouted.

I understood none of this, but something had awakened all my senses, sharpened them, and I felt united with all those people in their search for the perfect asparagus, the perfect shrimp, its blue-gray translucence a pearl beyond price.

"Why do you keep buying bread?" I asked Liz as we loaded everything into the trunk. They were driving Toni's cousins' Renault. On the key ring was a gadget that was smaller than a matchbox. It opened and closed the door locks from a distance of twenty feet. Infrared sensors, fifty different kinds of olives, but no shower curtains! "You bought two loaves for breakfast. There was still some left." These loaves were no bigger around than a baseball bat and about as long as a Louisville Slugger.

"It doesn't keep," she said.

"Good bread is something you buy for each meal," Toni chimed in, all Gallic assertiveness. "After two or three hours, forget it."

Once back at the house they set about making lunch. I took a book outside and tried to find a shady spot in which to stretch out. There was none. The sun raged down with such blinding intensity I had no difficulty at all in understanding why Van Gogh went mad while living in this country.

On one side of the blue pool was a white metal table with a collapsed umbrella growing through a doughnut hole punched through its center. I forced up the slide to open the ribs, but the umbrella was nothing but a wind-whipped faded red rag. I resolved to buy a patio umbrella tomorrow. It was high noon. There was no shade anywhere. The wind whistled through the ruined umbrella. There were four white metal chaises, all

too hot to touch. Where are the cushions? I wondered.
In New York there would be cushions.

I leaned against the stuccoed wall of the house,
standing in a miserable, ten-inch swath of shade and
wondered if coming here had been such a great idea after all. I could be fishing with Ross, I told myself. I could
be working a wet-fly down a reach of the Big Two-
Hearted River, slapping mosquitoes in the cold morning air. It struck me that sometimes it was a hard and
lonely business, loving a woman. Then I heard Liz
calling me to lunch.

She put her head out the French door, and the moment I saw her, my heart stopped with desire, my guts
melted. Her face and neck were glistening with trickling sweat; my T-shirt was pasted to her, darkly stained
between her breasts. The wispy hairs that framed her
face corkscrewed wildly. Droplets beaded her upper lip.
I wanted to lick them away. I wanted to carry her off to
a cool mossy cave, where the light was green, palely
filtered through limestone, and I could lick up all her
droplets everywhere, drink the very life of her.

I stepped through the door and she laid a hand on my
chest. She knew what I was thinking. "Later," she
whispered, leaning close enough to flick my lips with
the tip of her tongue. I snapped my teeth, but she was
too quick for me. Sweating hand in sweating hand, we
crossed the cool slate floor to the kitchen table.

While we ate, we chatted about inconsequential
things, but I could feel the unspoken resonance between Liz and Toni, as though each was listening for the
other's silent echo. Liz treated Toni as though at any
moment she might astonish us by exploding into a bil-
lion pieces, or by going exotically mad. I felt clumsy

beside them, awkward, as though I'd opened the wrong door and stumbled into a china shop.

Early afternoon was the hottest part of the day. The bedrooms were too hot to enter. All over the house, the shutters were closed against the heat; the house in half light seemed to be underwater. I took a book into the living room where the television stared blankly, and dozed off reading in a chair covered with itchy cut velvet. I could hear them talking in the kitchen, their voices following me like drowsy bees. As contented as lizards in that heat, they talked to each other in French, practicing. I often wondered if they were talking about me....

AS THE DAYS PASSED, I quickly came to love Avignon. It is an ancient walled city—a town, really—tucked into a tightish curve of the Rhône River, snug as a chick in an egg. The later additions, like Toni's cousins' house, are all outside the walls, a modern sprawl of houses, apartment buildings, supermarkets, and schools resting like gleaming white shells on the emerald carpets of their soccer fields. Tourists prowl the streets, fill the cafés, ride the carousel in the town square, visit the Pope's Palace, and the lumpish remains of the ruined bridge that once spanned the river. "Sur le Pont d'Avignon," even I had heard that song—tourists whistled it in the streets. I liked the old town best. To enter it we passed through ancient gates in the medieval walls. It was like being admitted to a secret.

In the days that followed, we drove to nearby towns, through gently rolling country dusted with silver-green olive groves, past orchards of espaliered fruit trees. Liz insisted I must see Cassis, so we drove over a hump of low mountains to the sea, where we walked the pebbled shore and ate bouillabaisse at a place they were fond of. *Absolutely authentic*, they said. *We guarantee it*, and it was good.

For me, everything was new and startling, but for Liz and Toni all these excursions were like trying on old clothes that have been stored over the winter, getting comfortable again. Their talk was all comparisons. Was it as good as last year? Papa René, the bouillabaisse genius, had finally retired; his son had taken his place. Was the son's sorbet as silken as his father's? Racing along the autoroute, following our yellow headlights back to the house on rue Mallarmé, they discussed the proper way to make a sorbet. The secret seemed to involve egg white.

I dozed in the back seat, half listening, thinking about the long history Liz and Toni shared, wondering about Liz's life before I came along. I hadn't given it much thought until the day we went to Arles.

We had spent the morning walking the hot dusty streets of Arles and visiting an exhibition of Van Gogh's paintings. They still had bullfights in the Roman amphitheater—bloodless ones. Ol' Hemingway would have hated that—but I was grateful. I'd seen enough blood to last me a lifetime.

Early evening found us back in Avignon, at a sidewalk café in a cobbled square. Liz and I were trying to wash the dust out of our throats with cold beer, Toni was sipping lime tea. It looked as though a thousand other weary travelers had all had the same brilliant idea at exactly the same moment. The tables beneath the dusty plane trees were jammed. Little children—as colorful as Chinese finches—swooped and dodged around the crowded chairs, shrieking with laughter. That, at least, is the same in any language.

"I'm exhausted," said Liz. "A cool shower and a swim and I'm going to crash."

"That makes two of us," said Toni. "Where do all these people come from? Just look at them all."

Three little kids, arms outstretched, flying low, buzzed our table. "Aiiieee!" they sang out as they dipped their wings.

Liz and I turned in our chairs to follow their ecstatic flight across the square. "I don't believe it," she said, nudging Toni with her elbow. "Look!"

"What?" I said.

"Oh, my God!" Toni said, following her pointing finger. "What's he doing here?"

"Who?" I said.

"Er...Michael," said Liz.

"Who's Michael?"

"Has he seen us?" said Toni.

"He was my stockbroker."

"I could use a good broker," I said. "I haven't got much, but whenever I call my guy he's out playing handball."

"You wouldn't want him," said Liz. "He's...um...not the sort of broker you can count on to give your account a lot of individual attention."

Toni sputtered into her tea. "He's seen you."

"No, he hasn't." Liz looked away.

"He's coming over."

"No, he's not."

"Hi!" said the man they called Michael. He wore khaki shorts, a pink polo shirt with one of those trendy polo players embroidered over his heart like a talisman and Mafia-black sunglasses. A white streak of zinc oxide melted on his nose. He looked to be in good shape. He looked as if he worked out five days a week and drank tiger's milk by the gallon, but every exposed inch of him, every laboriously sculpted muscle, was sunburned.

"Hello, Michael," said Liz. Her voice sounded doubtful. "This is Ben. Ben, Michael."

We smiled mechanically at each other. I didn't like the way he was looking at Liz. He looked at her as though he could see right through her clothes. She raked him with a glance that just managed to disguise defiance and contempt with a look of supreme indifference. That look alone should have told me all I needed to know, but I was a little slow on the uptake that afternoon.

"Sorry we can't ask you to sit down," said Toni, all sweetness and light, "but there don't seem to be any chairs, and we were just talking about going back to—"

"Yoohoo! Mikey, sweetie!" A blonde with a child's piping voice, banana-colored hair and more curves than a screwball pitcher, waved from the other side of the square. There wasn't a man or boy within a hundred yards who didn't follow her with his eyes as she swivel-hipped her way between the crowded tables to Michael's side. She wore skimpy pink shorts and a skimpier tank top that she must have sprayed on. Black sunglasses like Michael's were perched on her tiny nose. She was a real, live, walking, talking centerfold.

"You naughty boy," she was saying to Michael. "I couldn't figure out where you'd gotten to."

"This is Candy," said Michael. *I'll bet she is*, I thought as he introduced her all around.

"I looked for you all over, sugar." Candy pushed her lower lip out as she said this. It was a pout she must have practiced for hours in front her makeup mirror. It had its desired effect on Michael. He looked as though he might melt into the dust at her feet.

She canceled her pout and turned a confiding smile on Liz and Toni. "I had to find a 'ladies.' Don't you just love the new loos they've put up all over Paris? The ones that look like little silver spaceships? And they play music! Aren't the French just too wonderful. For two francs I got old-fashioned American hygiene and a tape of some woman singing a weepy ballad."

Toni crossed her eyes at Liz, and Liz jumped up, saying, "Why don't you take our table. We were just leaving."

Toni pushed her chair back just as a waiter bustled up, carrying two chairs high over his head.

"Sit down," said Michael to Liz. "Stay, and have a drink." He turned to me. "You want another drink?"

"Why not?" I said. I was still thirsty. One beer isn't enough to wash away a day's dust.

Liz and Toni shot me looks that said I was being a real jerk, but I was thirsty. Besides, the look Liz had given Michael had stirred my curiosity. Who would lavish a look of defiance, contempt, and indifference on an ex-stockbroker? An ex-lover? As I saw it, I had every right to be curious.

Liz sat down, and the waiter tried to place both chairs between Liz and me, but Michael snatched one and set it down on the other side of me, facing Liz, but about as far from her as he could get. He sat down looking pleased with himself, but wary. We all ordered beer.

"So," said Michael brightly, his black glasses turning from Liz to Toni and back. "Still coming to Avignon, I see. You look great, Liz. Both of you look great. So, how've you been? How's the foot?"

"Fine," said Liz. "Just fine. We really should be going."

"What happened to your foot?" I said. What kind of stocks did this guy push that he knew about Liz's feet?

"I broke it."

"How?" I said.

"It looks great," said Michael, studying her foot under the table.

Candy twisted a lock of yellow hair around her finger and leaned—bosom and all—toward me. It was startling, like facing twin torpedoes. "Are you in the fillum business, too?" She pronounced the word "film" as if it had two syllables.

"No. I'm just an editor." Fire one! Fire two!

"Tabloids?" she said hopefully.

"Books."

"I'm not much into books." She turned back to Michael.

"It doesn't look as though you'd been in a cast or anything," he was saying.

"Do you mean you really broke your foot?" I said.

"She sure did," said Michael.

"A turkey fell on it," Toni offered in that mysterious, baffling way women have.

"C'mon, Liz," I said. "What really happened?"

She smiled at me so sweetly, so tenderly, I knew she was ready to cut me off at the kneecaps if I brought up the subject again. "Trust me," she murmured to me, though her glance darted at Toni. "It was a turkey."

Toni stepped in right on cue. "And what have you been up to, Michael? Still selling junk bonds?"

"Hey! I never sold junk bonds." He took a long pull on his beer. "I've gone into public relations. I represent Candy."

Liz arched an eyebrow at him. "In Avignon?"

"We're on our way to the film festival down on the Riviera." He pushed his glasses up on top of his head and squinted at me, darting pale glances from me to Liz to Toni and back to me. He was trying to decide which one I was with. "Been here long?"

"Seems like minutes," I said. What business was it of his? I decided to needle him a little. "Liz and Toni have been showing me the sights. Giving me the insider's tour, you might say. We've been having one helluva time."

"Have we?" he said. "And how's Ned?" he asked Toni, a nasty edge on his voice. Who was this guy, anyway, that he knew Ned? I'd never even met the infamous Ned.

"He's on the Coast making a pilot," I said, sending him a look that said the subject is closed.

But he wasn't receiving. Or, maybe he was just plain nasty. "It must be a real treat for the two of you—playing house with John-Boy here. A real *ménage à trois*. Isn't that what they call it?"

"Ben, not John-Boy," said Liz evenly.

Michael leaned toward me—very buddy-buddy, very confiding. "Wait until football season, fella. You can take it from me, this lady turns into a real witch." He pointed his chin at Liz. "The other one probably turns into her cat."

Liz's eyes opened so wide they looked like two em-
eralds on white plates, her hand twitched and scrab-
bled on the table as though it had a life of its own. I
reached for her hand. It was an automatic thing, the
kind of instinctive gesture anyone would make to
comfort a wounded creature. Somehow I clipped Michael's beer with my elbow and it poured all over the
poor, unlucky S.O.B.

"I don't believe it," he squeaked, leaping up and
trying to shake the cold beer from his lap. "You planned
this, didn't you? You two are in cahoots." He meant Liz
and Toni.

A half smile flickered across Liz's mouth, and Toni
raised one evil eyebrow.

"C'mon, honey, let's go," said Candy.

He pulled down his sunglasses and flashed them at
me. "Go ahead, fella. You just get her to tell you about
the turkey."

"Ooow, c'mon!" Candy pulled him away.

We watched him flee across the square with Candy
in his wake. He dodged through the crowds like a bro-
ken-field runner, dragging poor Candy by the wrist.

I turned back to Liz. "Who exactly was that guy?"

"American hygiene!" Toni snorted. "Who does she
think Louis Pasteur was—a rock band?"

"So who was that guy?"

Liz said, "He's just someone I used to know a long,
long time ago. So long ago he's ancient history." To her
credit, there was such puzzlement in her voice, it was
clear she couldn't remember why she'd ever liked him,
if that's what the ancient history was between them.

"Did breaking your foot have something to do with
football? Were you playing tag football with him in

Central Park? Did you trip over a turkey?" I was having a tough time making sense out of the few facts I'd been given.

"Nothing like that, darling. You're not even close. It's really a very boring story, and hardly worth telling."

"I'd like to hear it," I said firmly.

She looked at me hard. A look that said, *Don't push me*, and then she lashed out, green eyes blazing, in that astonishing way women do when they take it into their heads that the best defense is a good offense.

"I don't have to justify my past to you. Okay? I knew him once. Isn't that enough?"

But suddenly it wasn't. "Knew? What do you mean—knew?"

"We lived together. Is that what you wanted to hear? Well, now you've heard it. Do you want to hear about our sex life?"

"Let's go home," said Toni to Liz, pleading. To me she snarled, "Liz doesn't have to take this from you."

"And who the hell are you? Liz's self-appointed guardian angel? I'm her lover, who are you?"

"I'm her friend," she said, her eyes blazing.

I DROVE BACK IN SILENCE as thick and unyielding as cement. Toni rushed into the house. Liz and I sat in the car, miserable and a little scared. She looked down at her hands curled in her lap as though she didn't recognize them as her own. I turned on the radio, turned it off.

"I'm sorry," I said. "You were right about that guy being none of my business. Part of me knows that. But . . . Liz, I love you so much, I guess I just got jealous. Maybe I'm afraid of losing you. I don't know. But

I want to hoard you, keep you all to myself. I hate sharing you—with your past, with Toni."

"Toni needs me," she said to her hands.

"You can't devote your life to nursing lame ducks. If you do that, you won't have a life left."

"That's what friends are for."

"With the walking wounded, it's all take and no give. All you do, Liz, is give, give, give."

"You get something back when you give. Why can't men understand that? With men everything is a balance sheet, but friendship isn't cost-effective. There is no bottom line. It's not a matter of what's in it for me."

"Can't you see that Toni's a borderline neurotic, and you're not a shrink."

"How can you call my best friend neurotic?"

"You told me yourself that Ned was no good for her. If she's not neurotic, why has she been stumbling around like a lovesick Juliet? And why is she clinging to you?"

"You don't know the first thing about women and self-esteem. She's asking herself, *If I can't even hold a jerk like Ned, what kind of woman am I?*"

"But that's ridiculous. That's neurotic."

"That's never kept any woman from believing it."

NO ONE WANTED TO EAT. No one wanted to talk. Toni disappeared into the living room. Liz sat down at the kitchen table and ostentatiously opened a book.

"Liz," I began, "I want to talk."

"Not to me." She regarded me steadily, coolly. "Not now. I don't want to talk to you. I don't want to talk to Toni. I don't want to talk to anyone."

I found Toni curled up on the living-room couch staring at the blank TV screen.

"Look," I said, "I'm sorry I said those things."

"That's okay." She didn't look up.

"I'm afraid it was jealousy talking. I know that doesn't excuse it..."

"That's okay."

"...I just want you to know I'm truly deeply sorry."

She looked up at me then with eyes a little extra bright and a bitter-sad smile on her lips. "We're never going to be the Three Musketeers, are we?"

I walked out to the garden to pace around the pool and wonder how I could get through to Liz if she wouldn't talk to me. Finally, I threw myself into a chaise where I could lie back and watch the stars whirling in the blue-black sky. Provence had been working its magic on me. Isolated without language, I had found all my senses heightened as though I'd taken some psychedelic drug. Scents assailed me as they blew in from the hillsides: lavender and wild thyme, rosemary and savory. Everything on my tongue awakened new flavors. Every taste was as the first time—an astonishing discovery. Colors vibrated with shimmering intensity in the hot windy air.

Even my experience of Liz was a rediscovery. There was a new freedom, an abandon in her lovemaking that urged me to give myself over to my senses. She kept a bowl of apricots in our bedroom because she loved the scent: they throbbed with a perfume like love distilled. We ate them in bed, the warm thick juices trickling down our chins, over our fingers to be lapped and licked and sucked clean. Her skin beneath my fingers was always moist. Her body had a new perfume of pool water and jasmine soap. She wore jasmine blossoms in her hair at night, their crushed petals perfuming our bed. I was in an almost constant state of excitement from the first whiff of the day. Our afternoon kisses were flavored with salt and wine, but at night her tongue hid the honey of apricots, and when she was ready for love she tasted of sweet salty cream.

Liz and Toni had spent long hours in the sun, their bodies smeared with perfumed oils. Toni was the color of toast, Liz flushed with gold like her apricots. Her breasts were like rare fruit, renewed even as I devoured them. Her mouth, the teasing promise which I pursued through the day, became at night a passionate organ of fulfillment. Her throat was a cool column, its base inviting kisses. When we made love her hands fluttered across my back like mating birds, and I entered her as she opened for me, sighing her love. Then we were both fumed with desire, and her slim hips rocked beneath me to a rhythm as old as the sea, and love sang in my veins.

Thinking about Liz was a mistake. I wanted her so much I finally had to strip off my clothes and dive into the pool to cool myself down. I swam laps, back and forth, back and forth, willing her to come out to me. The light in the living room went out, leaving the garden in darkness. I could hear Toni climbing the wooden stairs to bed. The back door opened, and Liz stood tall in a shaft of moonlight, her nakedness magical, a gift to the moon. A gift to me? Then she dived and swam toward me, cleaving the black water like a silver fish, scattering the reflected disk of the moon. In perfect agreement, each mirroring the other's rhythm, we swam back and forth, back and forth. The storm was over.

Liz flipped over, diving ahead and beneath me, sliding the length of her body beneath mine like a porpoise. I could feel her thighs brushing my chest, her breasts sliding beneath my stomach, her mouth confirming my desire. We broke the surface gasping for air, and laughing, we raced for the shallow end. Liz stood, the water streaming off her breasts, running in silver streams from her fingertips. She was my Cybele again, my goddess of the moon, silver-gold in the moonlight. The water all around us was moonshot, glittering like the droplets I kissed from her eyelashes, the droplets I caught on my tongue as they fell from her breasts.

"Do you want to go in?" I said, my hands circling her waist, already urging her upward.

She smiled at me in answer and put her hand on me beneath the water. She was weightless when I lifted her, my naked silver fish, laughing as I raised her, her hands gripping my shoulders, and she sighed, "Oh, yes!" as I lowered her . . . my lover, my desire, my delight . . . as I lowered her . . . oh, yes!..lowered her onto me. Opening, closing, a fire of love she had for me. She opened for me and closed around me. Fire raced everywhere. We were both ablaze, opening and closing, thrusting deeper into the black velvety darkness, thrusting blindly into love, molten love, a swirling galaxy of love where we exploded together, a single white-hot star exploding across the surface of the water.

We clung to each other, exhausted, and then fell backward onto the water to float, hand in hand, gratefully on its moon-flecked surface. We were panting and laughing and when we kissed our mouths filled with water.

14

LAST NIGHT I WOKE UP in bed to realize Liz was not beside me. Then I saw them from the bedroom window, Liz and Toni, lying on air mattresses, floating in the pool. They were balancing glasses of wine on their stomachs and paddling with their feet, talking softly. They looked like lilies, naked in the moonlight. I lay back and watched a watery skein of reflected light dance flickeringly across the ceiling as I drifted toward sleep, thinking about their easy intimacy. As close as Ross and I have been, we'd have a tough time trying to talk to each other the way Liz and Toni do. I thought about Chuff and all the things we'd been able to tell each other—but only because we expected to be killed at any moment. And despite everything, we never talked about being afraid we might, ultimately, be cowards. All men, not just soldiers, are afraid of being cowards, but no one ever talks about it....

I dreamed that I was swimming at night in the sea, stroking smoothly through black water speckled with stars, when Liz and Toni swam up from beneath me, grabbed my ankles and pulled me under, down, down, through miles of choking black water.

Then Liz was shaking me awake. It was morning, and I was wanted on the phone—a call from New York. I took the call on the extension in the living room. Through the closed door I could hear Liz in the kitchen, making coffee. I heard the crunch of gravel that meant Toni was driving to the bakery for breakfast bread. By the time I hung up, she was back.

Liz and Toni looked up from the kitchen table, their faces expectant.

"Good news?" said Liz.

"I have to go back to New York," I said.

"What a shame," said Toni. She didn't even try to pretend she meant it.

"Oh, darling, no," said Liz. "But why?"

"Ross is in trouble. He needs my help."

"Yeah?" said Toni, biting into a croissant.

"Trouble? Ross? Then of course you must go. What's wrong?" said Liz. "Is there anything I can do?"

"No, it's something I have to handle myself. He asked me not to talk about it."

"You can't even tell us?" said Toni, her tone mocking and her ginger eyebrows climbing skeptically toward her hairline.

"'fraid not."

Liz searched my face. "Is it very serious?" I nodded, and her chair scraped back. "I'll help you pack."

"I'll find you a flight," said Toni, her hand already on the telephone directory. "Your best bet is Marseilles to Paris to New York."

As soon as we were alone, Liz said, "I'm sorry about Ross, whatever it is, but I can't leave Toni here all by herself. You understand that, don't you?"

"Of course I do. You should stay with her, she needs you." It wasn't easy, choosing exactly the right words. I wanted Liz to stay in Avignon. It was vital that she not come back to New York with me, or even worse, follow me back and pop up unannounced.

Liz

TONI AND I STOOD on the platform waving goodbye to Ben. Looking back down the tunnel of time, as one does, that was the moment when our friendship side-slipped crazily into another dimension.

He had given us both a parting kiss and a hug, in the hasty, slightly embarrassed way of travelers everywhere who long to be away. I was so self-absorbed, I never wondered what Toni might be thinking. Try as I might to put a good face on it, I still felt forlorn and more than a little sorry for myself. I was already brooding on how much I was going to miss him.

"Look at these tourists," Toni said, speaking in French, as we shouldered our way through the crowded station. She stumbled over a pile of knapsacks. I thought she was going to swear, but she laughed instead and cast her eyes toward heaven with a dramatic glance of passionate, heartbreaking despair.

"In another year or two," she said, "Avignon will be like Venice. Tour guides will funnel their hordes in one end and haul them out the other—an endless stream of foreigners. Where do they all come from? Well, I don't care, not today." We had reached the car park. "Look at that sky! Have you ever seen such a glorious sky? Is that a gorgeous blue, or is that a gorgeous blue?"

To my eye the sky was not blue at all, but a sulphurous hazy yellow-green.

"Let's walk over to Edouard's for lunch," she said, pocketing the car keys. "Let's have enormous plates of sausage and cornichons and glasses of icy beer." She was as manic and gay as I was depressed. "Let's have a

platter of sliced tomatoes with anchovies and onions
and a half-kilo of bread. Let's have . . ."

Bouncing along the street she planned our simple
lunch as though she'd been hired to cater for a crowned
prince. And when it came, the lunch was perfect, but
in my head a woman's voice sang all the old, sad songs.
Toni was laughing, munching sausage, joking with
Eduoard. I wanted to cry, which was a perfectly ridiculous, self-pitying sort of thing to want to do. I loathed
myself for it.

By the time we reached the car, Toni had stopped
bouncing around like Tigger. She was almost sub-
dued. She started the car, but didn't put it in gear.

"Liz, has Ben said anything more to you about why
he has to be back in New York? Anything that you
haven't told me?"

"No. What more is there to tell?"

"I wouldn't be your friend if I didn't tell you I think
that's the fishiest story I've ever heard." She was
breathing hard, and her hands trembled in her lap. "Ben
claiming he was to help out his ol' buddy Ross." She
punctuated her disbelief with her French shrug. "Ross
is in some sort of a jam? Give me a break. *Pa-leese!*"

"What are you getting at?"

"If I ever saw a man who seemed perfectly capable
of looking after himself, it's Ross."

"Who knows what kind of trouble Ross might be in?
Ben's not just his best friend, you know—he's his editor. Maybe it has something to do with a book."

"Is Ross working on a book?"

"I've no idea. Ben hasn't said anything about it."

"Well, there you are!"

"He must be working on a book. He's a writer, so I assume he's working on a book. What else would he be doing?"

"You assume a lot," she said, slamming the car into first and cannonballing across four lanes of traffic like a race-car driver.

"What's that supposed to mean?"

"Nothing. Forget it."

And that is where things stood until late that evening.

I'd taken my glass of wine outside so that I could stretch out on a chaise beside the pool. The wind had finally subsided and the air was suddenly oppressive, heavy with perfumes that urged all my senses toward love, but Ben was already so far away. I felt restless and uneasy. It was late and I was tired, but I didn't want to go in. I didn't want to climb the stairs to an empty bed. We would not whisper love-nonsense in the dark, our lips touching as we spoke. We would not sleep tonight with our love-spent bodies as tangled as vines.

The wine tasted sour. It was giving me a headache.

I wanted to tell him about the story I'd read that afternoon, the joke I'd heard on television, the confrontation between the pork butcher and the German tourists. I wanted Ben. That's what it came down to. I wanted Ben so much I couldn't think about anything else except wanting Ben. Had he really gone back to help out Ross? Why did I feel so uneasy about that? Granted we had not made any formal commitment to each other, but we were as close to that as we could possibly get without saying the actual words. We'd shared so much with each other. What was so confidential he had to tear himself, quite literally, from my arms with so little explanation? It shouldn't matter what it was. If I loved him, it went without saying that I trusted him. Didn't it?

Toni came out of the house. She walked the length of the rectangle of yellow light the living-room chandelier cast on the paving. She wore her peach-colored robe. As she stepped out of the light into the darkness beyond she dropped her robe and dived into the pool. We didn't speak. She swam back and forth for what seemed a long time. Sometimes I watched her, sometimes I watched the sky. I had already made up my mind not to go up to bed for another hour. The nights were going to seem endless now. Finally Toni climbed out. She lowered herself onto the chaise beside mine and toweled her face and hair.

I said, "You've never really liked Ben, have you?"

"Do you want me to be honest?"

"Of course I want you to be honest. We've never lied to each other."

"I think he's okay, but I'm not crazy about him."

"You hate him."

"I don't hate him. He's a very likable guy. I just don't trust him."

"But why not?"

"Because he's going to hurt you."

"Hurt me? Ben? That could never happen. He's the gentlest, most caring, most loving—"

"It's something I feel, Lizzie. I can feel it in my bones. You're going to get hurt."

"Then I'll get hurt. I'm a big girl. I can make my own decisions. Stop acting like a jealous mother hen, I'm not your chick."

"Let's just forget it, okay?"

How can you ever forget something like that? Your best friend tells you she doesn't trust your lover. Who could forget that? It was like the worm in the heart of the rose.

She reached out across the space that separated us. "Forgotten?"

"Forgotten," I said, taking her hand.

THE REST OF OUR TIME in Avignon was somehow off-pitch. Or like an old, familiar tune that's played on an inappropriate instrument, and in the wrong key. We did all the same things we'd always done, but we had to work so hard at enjoying ourselves that neither of us had much fun. I knew she was wrong. She knew she was right. And we, who had always talked about everything, never talked about it again.

15

I HOPED THAT BEN would meet our plane. Not that we'd planned it; on the contrary, we'd talked on the phone the night before, and since he hadn't mentioned it, I didn't bring it up, either. We hadn't talked of anything much really. Just "I miss you," and "I miss you, too," and "I went swimming last night," and "I wish I'd been there with you." It was all so ordinary and yet so full of love and desire I'm surprised we didn't melt the wires.

Somehow, we never got around to talking about his meeting the plane, which was probably just as well, because the plane was sure to be late, and then there's always the interminable wait for your luggage, on top of which you never know how long it's going to take to clear customs. On the other hand, I really had no one but myself to blame if Ben wasn't there. If I had wanted him to meet me, I should have asked him. And I hadn't, so that was that. I called him, though, as soon as Toni and I got home, but he wasn't in.

But when I walked into my office the next morning, it was like walking into a greenhouse—roses were massed everywhere: white ones on the desk, red ones on one windowsill, pink ones on the other, yellow ones on the file cabinets. And there was Ben, sitting in my chair with his feet up on my desk, the *Times* folded neatly on his lap. He was doing the crossword puzzle.

I don't know how I crossed the floor, perhaps I flew, but I was in his arms in an instant. We didn't even kiss, we just stood there without saying a word, holding each other as tightly as we could, happy in the wonder of being together again. When at last we did kiss, it seemed like so much more than an ordinary kiss. It was like a pledge, full of promise.

"Welcome home."

"Thank you for the flowers."

"I hope you like them. I was afraid it looked like a Mafia funeral."

"They're beautiful. Really."

"Busy tonight?"

"Yes, as a matter of fact, I am. I've got a heavy date with an editor I know..."

He kissed me once more in parting, but this time he started nibbling my lower lip. "Darling," I pleaded, pushing on his chest, "you promised you wouldn't do that at the office. You know it drives me crazy when you do that."

"Tonight." He spoke with his lips against mine.

"Oh, yes!" I had all I could do to keep my hands from urging him on.

As soon as he was out the door, I pulled myself together and called Toni. "'Roses, roses, everywhere...'"

"'And myrtle in my path like mad.'"

"I tell you, Ben is just plain wonderful. How I do adore that man. You've got to see what he's done to my office. The place looks like a Mafia funeral."

"Wait till you see mine, or better yet, smell it. Your Ben has filled it with carnations. How did he know I like carnations, did you tell him?"

"If I did, I don't remember. Sometimes I think he has a sixth sense. I wanted to tell you I have a heavy date tonight with a certain editor, so don't worry when I don't come home."

"You'll be at Ben's."

"With bells on."

By seven o'clock that night I'd only begun to make a dent in the mountain of work on my desk, but by then Ben was standing in my doorway with a half smile playing devilishly on his mouth and all but licking his lips. I grabbed the first thing to hand, which happened to be a coffee mug, to mark my place in the manuscript I was working on, locked my desk, and was out of my office in ten seconds flat.

We started kissing in the cab, and we didn't stop until the cab pulled up at Ben's apartment. We kissed in the elevator. To my mind, we were behaving just like all French lovers who kiss whenever and wherever the spirit moves them, but I'm afraid we scandalized a stuffy matron whose little boy tugged at her skirt and trilled, "Look, Mommie! They're kissing. Look, Mommie! The lady has her hand in his pocket."

We laughed all the way to Ben's bed where we tossed our clothes in the air and fell on each other like the love-starved animals we were. We made love as though we'd been apart for years rather than weeks. We growled and moaned, we nibbled and laughed, strewing passionate love bites everywhere. We caressed and stroked, squeezed and pushed and tasted, devouring each other in a delirium of desire.

THIS TIME IT WAS MY TURN to suffer from jet lag. My body was still running six hours ahead on French time, and it hit me an hour later in the shower as a warm gray fog dropped over me like a veil. Ben was giving my shoulders a soothing soap massage, his hands all slippery and slithery straying deliciously, now here, now there. I rested my head against his chest, closed my eyes for just a second, and the next thing I knew I was in Ben's arms and he was carrying me back to bed.

"You're asleep on your feet," he said.

"No, I'm not. I want to make love again. Don't turn the light off, I love watching you make love."

"Next thing you'll want a mirror on the ceiling."

"Hmm. Kiss me."

"Nap first. I don't want you conking out in the middle. It's very diminishing to the male ego to have a woman fall asleep in the middle."

"I take it you speak from experience."

That's when he dropped me onto the bed. I bounced like a tennis ball.

"Strictly hearsay." He stretched out beside me, my lover, the most beautiful man I'd ever seen, the most exciting man I'd ever known, and he gently brushed the damp hair away from my face. "Sleep now," he whispered, his lips against my ear.

"It's so good to be back." I settled my head on his shoulder. "Did you get that problem of Ross's sorted out?"

"Sleep now."

"Did you?"

"Almost."

"Kiss me again."

"I do like the way you . . ."

"Yes."

AT FOUR THE NEXT MORNING I was as wide-eyed as Little Orphan Annie, and Ben was not beside me. I got up expecting to find him in the living room, reading, but the apartment was dark. He wasn't there. Why would he go out without telling me? Where would he go? I went back to bed where I tossed and turned for what seemed like hours.

Ben's kisses woke me hours later. "Time to get up, sleepyhead." He was shaved and dressed.

"I can't move. Let's play hooky." I stretched languorously. "Your tongue tastes like a cinnamon stick. Kiss me again." This he obligingly did. Finally, I sat up. "I just remembered. You ran out on me. I woke up in the middle of the night, and you weren't here."

"Of course I was here."

"I looked all over for you. I couldn't have missed you, you've only got two rooms."

"You must have been dreaming. Jet lag does funny things to people."

But I hadn't been dreaming. At least I was eighty-five percent sure I hadn't been dreaming.

MY PHONE WAS RINGING when I opened my office door. It was Toni. "Come on down," she whispered. "We've got to talk."

"Why are you whispering."

"Hurry," she said and hung up.

I didn't wait for the elevator, I took the stairs. On the landing Paul and Lars were so deep in earnest conversation they didn't even see me.

Toni said, "Did you wake up early? Practically the middle of the night?" I nodded. "Jet lag. So did I, and I knew I'd never get back to sleep so I came into work."

I started to tell her about Ben not being there, and then being there, but she held up her hand like a traffic cop. "You know the security guard? The one who's supposed to be in the lobby all night? Well, he wasn't in the lobby. He had taken the elevator down the basement—for safety purposes, no doubt—and switched it off. I think he makes himself pots of coffee down there. Anyway, I started up the stairs, and almost immediately I heard someone in the stairwell just above me—"

"In the stairwell? What time did you say this was?"

"Around four-thirty, but the important thing is that I distinctly heard the door to your floor close. It has that piggy squeal, you know? So, I crept up the stairs, and pushed the door open just far enough to peek through, and there was Ben—"

"No!"

"I only saw his back, but I'm sure it was Ben. He was letting himself into Paul's office."

"He couldn't have been!"

"I saw him. He had a key."

"There must be some reasonable explanation."

"Yeah? Like what?"

"It wasn't Ben at all. It was one of Paul's writers. It wouldn't be the first time he's let a writer sleep on his office couch. Everyone knows what a soft touch he is. He once let a writer camp out on his couch for months when he was dead broke. I thought he was going to get away with it forever, but Mr. Pomfret caught him at it."

"Do you really think that's who it was?"

"Of course I do. It's the only explanation."

"Then all we have to do is ask Paul."

"He'd never admit he was letting one of his writers use his office again. You know how loyal he is to his writers, how protective. Besides, Mr. Pomfret warned him that he'd fire him if he ever caught him at it again."

The more I thought about it in the days that followed, the more certain I became that Ben was probably right, that my conviction that he'd left me that night was no more than a jet-lag induced fantasy. As though to underscore this, life at the Press seemed to run along fairly smoothly in its normal groove, its normal groove being a state of genteelly controlled hysteria that passes for everyday life in the world of publishing.

I did notice, though, that Mr. Pomfret looked pale and rather frazzled. He summoned me to his office one morning to ask, in whispers, if I knew anything about bound review galleys going out to reviewers with whole signatures—that is sections—missing. I told him I didn't.

"It's very vexing," he said. "Couldn't be accidental?"

I shook my head sadly. But though I waited apprehensively for something more to happen, nothing did, and I had my own work to worry about.

In fact, we all had more work at the Press than we could complete in three lifetimes. Almost every evening found me working late, then falling exhausted but happy into Ben's arms, curling into the curve of his body where I felt as cozy as a thumb in a mitten. I'd fall asleep instantly to the slow even rhythm of his breathing, only to be sweetly wakened by my morning lover, ready for love.

My lover. Is there anything more warming to the cockles of a woman's heart than to find herself wakened by the man she adores, already roused? My lover. If sometimes you wonder how they do it, those women you see striding down Madison Avenue in the morning, briefcases swinging, eyes glittering, their faces radiant as angels, I'll tell you. It's not a guise you can duplicate with cunning makeup, a look you can mimic with a glamour-girl haircut and the right suit. No. They glow like that because they made love this morning. You have to have a good lover to look like that. And I, on my way to work, glowed with a vengeance. No woman has given out so much candlepower since they electrified the torch on the Statue of Liberty.

The more time I spent with Ben, the more comfortable I felt; the more at ease he made me feel, the easier it became to dismiss Toni's belief that she had seen Ben at Paul's door as either a case of mistaken identity, or even a figment of her operatic imagination.

My imagination was entirely occupied with my life with Ben. That's how I thought of it, and it was like entering into a whole new life. At the Press, though with one thing and another we often didn't catch sight of each other all day, we sometimes managed to meet for a brown-bag lunch. But always we tried to spend as many evenings together as we could, and of course as many nights.

I don't for a moment imagine one of our typical evenings together would look romantic to a twenty-year-old, but they were everything to me. The perfect still center of my life. After work we'd grab something to eat, go back to his place, put on a pot of coffee, kick off

our shoes, put our feet up on the coffee table and work
on manuscripts.

"You're humming again, darling."

"Am I? Sorry."

"What was that tune?"

"What tune?"

"The one you were humming."

"I don't know, I wasn't listening."

Perhaps the nicest, most gratifying thing about being
with Ben was that I didn't have to pretend, I didn't have
to wear a mask. I never felt I had to create a special per-
sona just for Ben—make myself over into another sort
of woman to fulfill his fantasy of me. To feel this free,
this comfortable with a man was truly a liberating experience for me. I felt so easy with him I even brought
over my "security robe" and hung it on the back of his
bathroom door. This is a flannel robe that was once—
in a far, far distant past—a rich, dark green plaid. It is
now as pale as moss and thin as voile, but I love it beyond all reason. In some deep-seated primitive way
which I choose not to analyze, home is where I hang my
robe.

Looking back, I know now that things had reached
a point where I was more comfortable with Ben than
with Toni. Toni so often found some way of getting at
Ben; that is, when she talked. All too often she didn't
talk at all, and an evening at home would be spent with
Toni watching a video of *Sunset Boulevard* with stereo
headphones on, while I worked on a manuscript. These
evenings were as cold as the witch's proverbial with-
ers. No joy there, let me tell you. Who could blame me
for wanting to spend every free moment with Ben? On
the other hand, when Toni and I met Drew and Chris

for our usual sushi bash, Toni put on a public face and behaved pretty much as she always did.

"It's over," said Chris, as soon as we'd ordered. "Memmo and I are over. I've sold my health club membership and enrolled in a history of feminism course at the New School."

"What happened?"

Chris sighed and slipped her chopsticks from their paper wrapper. "He started asking me if he could borrow money."

"Oh, no!"

"Did you give him any?"

"Wrong-o!"

"How much did you give him?"

She waved the questions away, her distracted fingers folding and refolding the paper wrapper. "I finally hired a detective to check up on him."

"You didn't!"

"Wow!"

"I didn't really know that much about him, did I? Just that he worked at the club and was great in bed. He said he'd been to Dartmouth, but had dropped out to write plays. How was I supposed to know if what he told me was true? Lots of women are doing it—hiring detectives, checking up on guys—what else can we do these days? We have to look out for ourselves, don't we?"

"There's no one else to do it," said Toni, and we all agreed to that.

"He has a wife and two kids. A wife and two kids." Her voice was harsh. "Men!" she said bitterly. She looked with surprise at the folded paper in her fingers. She set it carefully beside her plate, a perfect origami male organ. She rested her chopsticks on it.

Mercifully, the sushi arrived, and Drew said, "I've got to tell you about this cake. It's called 'The Cake That's Better Than Sex.' My secretary brought it into the office. It's divine. I kid you not." She sipped her tea with her eyes closed, remembering the cake. "It's very simple. Anyone can make it. All you need is yellow cake mix, lemon pudding mix and canned pineapple, and when it's baked you sprinkle shredded coconut on the icing...."

Toni crossed her eyes at me, and I grinned back. The two of us connected, and it was just like it's always been. Toni carried on a one-woman crusade against mixes. Pizza from a carton, yes. Yellow cake mix? She'd rather go to the guillotine first.

"Toni," Drew was saying, "do you think you want to try it? My secretary's already offered to type up the recipe."

"*Moi?* When it comes to cakes I always follow Miss Piggy's advice. 'Never eat all of anything in one sitting that you cannot lift.'"

Drew dug around in her purse, cleared her throat and handed each of us a slip of paper. "My new phone number and address. I'm moving in with Pavel."

"Why?"

"Because we're in love, of course. It just doesn't make any sense to live apart, to maintain two places. Not when he's got this great apartment near Columbia— wonderful old building, high ceilings..."

And while they talked I thought about Ben and me. How long could I go on this way? Did I want to go on, living as I was in two places at once, shuttling back and forth. I looked up from my plate. Toni was watching me. She was reading my thoughts as clearly as though they'd been printed on my forehead in three-inch bold-faced caps. After dinner, we said good-night to the others and flagged a cab. I wanted to talk, but it's impossible to have a meaningful conversation in a taxi vibrating to a reggae beat.

"Do we have any fruit?" I said, locking our door behind us. Toni was sorting her mail from mine and tossing the magazines into the dough-bowl on the foyer table. "What I wouldn't give for a kilo of fresh apricots."

"Look in the fridge. In case you've forgotten, that's the large white thing in the kitchen. The one that rumbles. The silent white thing is the stove. Should your memory fail you, the kitchen is straight back down that hall."

I didn't go to the kitchen in search of fruit. I said, "I gather this is your not very subtle way of pointing out that I haven't been around much lately."

"You got it in one. Give the lady a cigar!"

"But I've been with Ben," I said, an explanation that appeared to explain nothing and to mitigate less.

"I went to the concert alone last night."

"Oh, my God! The art songs! I completely forgot. I'm sorry, I really am sorry."

"We've been going to that series on the third Tuesday of every month for more than a year. How could you forget?"

"I just did. Ben and I went home and read scripts."

"Home? I thought this was your home?"

"It is. It is my home," I sputtered, flustered and irritated.

"I thought we had a life. Together. As friends. I'm not your friend anymore, I'm the person who brings up your mail."

"Toni, I missed one concert. One concert. It's not the end of the world."

"It's symptomatic. I don't have a place in your life anymore...."

"But you do!"

"As what? Landlord? Postal assistant? You're going to go, aren't you? You're going to move out. You're going to move in with Ben and leave me. You never talk to me anymore. We don't share things anymore. What's happened to us? Liz, if I lose you I won't have anything left."

I didn't know what to say. I didn't have a line of cheerful patter ready to counter what amounted to emotional blackmail. "You're not going to lose me. Toni, I'd never desert you. You ought to know that after all this time."

"Then why don't I believe you?"

"I don't know."

"You love Ben, that's why. I've seen you through affairs before, but never one like this. I've never seen you like this."

"I've never loved anyone the way I love Ben."

"That was obvious from the moment I discovered you'd taken your old green robe."

"Why are you always looking for signs and portents? I needed a robe, that's all. Ben's are much too big."

"You don't know what it's like to come home to an empty apartment. When you're at Ben's I wander around, and the place gives me the creeps. I go from room to room turning on all the lights. And if I cough, it echoes. It does. You didn't know this place echoes, did you? I turn on the stereo, and the television in the kitchen, and the radio in the shower, and still I can hear it echo. What am I supposed to do? Buy a cat?"

"You're allergic to cats."

"Why are you so desperate to live with Ben when he's not exactly leaping at the chance? We've got a great life here. We've been happy together, I know we have. Why can't we go on like this? Sleep over there if that's what you want to do, but live here. That's what Ben wants."

"How do you know that?"

"That's what every man wants—sex without responsibility."

"Ben's not like that."

"Every man is like that. Has Ben ever said one single word to you about moving in?"

"No, but I've never mentioned it to him, either." But I want to, I said to myself. Oh, how I want to.

"Then maybe it's time you did. You'll find out just how serious he really is. Go ahead. Ask him. I dare you."

"You *dare* me?" Suddenly I was shaking with fury.

"You haven't got the guts to ask him about anything that means a real commitment. You're afraid to ask him, aren't you?"

"I most certainly am not," I said. I grabbed my purse and headed for the door.

Toni jumped up and started to follow me. "Where do you think you're going? We haven't finished talking."

I opened the door and turned, my hand on the knob. "Can't you see how ridiculous this is?"

"I fail to see anything ridiculous in our talking this over."

"This isn't talking. This is a stupid argument. If you saw us on stage you'd call it a comedy."

"You think we're a comedy?"

"Yes," I snapped. I was already heading for the elevator when I heard her shout after me.

"You always did love a good exit line. If you think we're a comedy, here's another for you: *La commedia è finita!*"

16

BY THE TIME I REACHED Ben's door I knew exactly what
I was going to say. There was no reason to be nervous.
After all, Ben and I loved each other—we'd whispered
our love a thousand times. "I love you," he'd mutter out
of the corner of his mouth as he passed me at the office.
"I love you," I'd say as we nibbled Chinese take-out in
bed. "Love you...love you...love you..." we said
together when we made love. We were of one mind on
so many things, surely he would agree that the time had
come for us to...to what, exactly? Make our tacit
pledge a fact, I suppose.

I pressed Ben's bell and arranged my face in a smile
that said, *Surprise*. The door opened about six inches.

"Liz!"

"Hello, darling."

"Liz!"

"You're surprised to see me."

"Yes. I never expected—"

"Aren't you going to ask me in, darling?"

"In?"

"Yes, in. Technically speaking, my side of the door
is called, out. Your side of the door is called, in."

"Yes, of course. Come in, come in."

I walked past him to the living room and sat down.

He perched on the arm of the chair across from me,
his hands on his knees. "Well. Here you are."

"Yes."

"Why?" he said.

"What kind of question is that for a lover to ask?"

"What I mean is, what brings you here at this time of night?" He glanced at his watch. "I thought you were out with your pals stuffing yourself with sushi."

"That was hours ago. Are you feeling all right?"

"Of course I'm all right. Don't I look all right?"

"You're dithering." Then it struck me. "Are you alone? Is there someone here with you?" In spite of myself I had a shockingly vivid image of Candy—Michael's nubile tootsie—all dewy, eager and oh, so terribly, terribly young, spread-eagled on Ben's bed.

"That question," he said haughtily, squaring his shoulders and tucking in his chin, "does not deserve to be dignified with an answer."

"Is she here?" I didn't want to ask, but I couldn't help myself.

"Who, she?"

"Candy."

He blinked at me.

"Surely you remember Candy. The blond bombshell Michael was repping in Avignon. I can't believe you've forgotten her so soon. You were positively slavering into her cleavage."

"She was trash!" He rubbed his eyes wearily. "You're obsessed. Do you know that? You'd got it into your head that some teenager is going to throw me over her handlebars and pedal off into the sunset. I am not interested in younger women!" He was very nearly shouting. "Frankly, women that age bore me."

"Then you don't have another woman here."

"I swear to you, I do not have another woman here."

"Then why have you been practically twitching ever since I came in? You haven't even kissed me."

"I haven't? Are you sure?"

"Ben . . . darling. . . . Isn't it just possible that my obsession, as you insist on calling it, is really a symptom?" I took a deep breath and plunged in. "I came here tonight because I think it's time we talked. . . ."

"This is not a good time . . ."

" . . . time we discussed where we're going . . ."

"Couldn't be a worse time . . ."

" . . . how our relationship is evolving . . ."

"Worst possible time, in fact."

"You haven't heard a word I said. I want to talk about us."

"This is not a good time to bring this up."

"There'll never be a better time to talk about us."

"What's wrong with us?" He slid sideways off the arm and folded himself into the chair with an air of resignation. "If you ask me, we've got a pretty good life. In fact, it strikes me as the perfect relationship. I don't want it to evolve. I like it just the way it is. It's a great life."

"But look at the way we live. This isn't a life, it's an affair. I don't want an affair, Ben. I want a real life, not a pretend one. A life based on some kind of real commitment to each other. I'm tired of other people's stories, other people's fantasies."

"What is it, exactly, that you want?"

"I want a life that goes on after the last chapter."

He glanced at his watch, sighed, and leaned forward, his elbows on his knees, the very image of a patient man attempting to awaken reason in a disordered mind. It was infuriating. "Liz, my dear, life is not a novel where all the tangles are straightened out in the last chapter. Life is a muddle. All we can do is try to make the best—"

"Don't patronize me, Ben Malloy. I didn't ask you for your philosophical views on the meaning of Life with a cap *L*—"

"Dammit, Liz. I tried commitment once. It didn't work. I've been a loner ever since. You've known that from the beginning. I told you."

"Be reasonable, darling. That was almost twenty years ago. You're not the same person now you were then, at least I hope you're not. You were still a kid. What kind of meaningful commitment can a kid make?"

"I love you, and I swear I'll never do anything to hurt you. Isn't that enough?"

"No, it's not enough. Do you think I don't know there's a secret part of your life you won't let me into, won't talk about? Rushing back to New York from Avignon like that, and then sneaking out of bed and pretending you'd never been away."

Ben cleared his throat and stared at the floor in front of him.

"I want to share your life, not just your soap-on-a-rope. A shared life is based on trust. On really living together."

"I haven't lived with anyone for twenty years."

"Not once? Not even for a week?"

"No."

"What about a weekend?"

"Maybe a weekend. Here and there. Along the way..."

"What's wrong with you that no woman can live with you for seven consecutive days?"

"There's nothing wrong with me. There have been dozens of women who were dying to live with me."

"Then why haven't they?"

"Because I've never asked them. I've never been able to see myself yoked to another person. I'm a loner, not a team player. Why do we have to live together? We sleep together almost every night."

"What do you mean 'almost'?"

"You've been here ten out of the last fourteen nights. The other four nights you were home with Toni."

"What are you doing—keeping score? Notching your pistol?"

"You're talking nonsense." His eyes strayed toward his wrist again.

"Why do you keep looking at your watch?"

"I have an appointment."

"With whom?"

"I'm sorry. I can't tell you."

"You see, that's just what I mean. Secret meetings. Midnight assignations."

"It's only eleven." He stood up. "I've got to go. I was just going out when you came."

"That's all you have to say?"

"For the moment, yes."

"Toni was right."

"Isn't she always?"

"I'm going to pretend I didn't hear that. She said sex without responsibility is what every man wants."

"That sounds like Toni. I'm sorry, Liz, I just don't have time to discuss this now, I have to go."

"If you walk out of here without any explanation, without telling me where you're going, don't expect me to be here when you get back. In fact, I'm not at all sure I'll ever again want to be here when you get back."

"You don't mean that."

"You bet your buttons I mean it."

He shrugged into his jacket and left me without so much as a backward glance.

It's an awful thing to admit, but the first thing I did when the door closed was flip on the light in the bedroom. No sign of Candy. No sign of anyone except Ben and me. I don't know what got into me, but just to be sure, I looked in his closets. I even peeked behind his shower curtain. I sat on the edge of the tub tying knots in his soap-on-a-rope, and wondering if I had meant what I'd said. Was it over? How could he turn my questions away like that? Why couldn't he trust me? Was I so blinded by love, such a fool for love that I was willing to pursue a love not grounded in trust? Where would it lead?

I had a lot of thinking to do, and I could hardly do it at Ben's apartment when I'd just sworn I wouldn't be there waiting for him. I couldn't go home, because I didn't want to talk to Toni. This isn't a city where a woman can safely walk the streets at night while she tries to sort through her troubled thoughts. I flagged a cab and went across town to an Indian restaurant I know where a woman can feel comfortable dining alone.

I don't know how long I sat at the bar, crumbling poppadoms onto a saucer and barely tasting a glass of wine, but it must have been a long time. I had so many conflicting things I needed to think about. I knew what I wanted. I wanted Ben. Ben period. Ben permanently. But how could I make him change his mind? I wanted a life with a future that stretched beyond the end of the week. It was the long view I was taking now, and that longest view of all reached all the way to marriage. Well, why not? As far as I could see, it was all pluses and no minuses. But did I really want that? Now? After all this time? Yes! Did I want to give up my freedom? I tried to make a list of the freedoms I would be losing if I was to marry Ben, but I didn't come up with much.

But what good was it wanting to get married, if Ben wouldn't even consider living together? How could I persuade him that our best hope for a real future was in marriage? Maybe if we stopped seeing each other for a while, he'd realize how much he needed me. On the other hand, he might realize he could get along without me. But wasn't he the one who had insisted on coming to Avignon? Hadn't we been closer than ever since those glorious weeks? On the other hand, what about his secretive side? How could we have a marriage without trust? We couldn't.

And then there was Toni. There had to be some way for her to stand on her own two feet without leaning on me. Ned's running out on her had been a devastating blow to her self-esteem, but now that she was more or less her old self again, I felt trapped with her. I thought of the fox in the fable who gnawed off his own paw to escape the hunter's trap. Our friendship had been so important to me for so long. Would I have to cut off a part of myself to escape it?

Mr. Mohan broke into my thoughts. "We're closing now, Miss. I've called a taxi for you. It's waiting at the door." He smiled sweetly, gold teeth flashing. "Hard thoughts become easier after a little sleep. You'll see."

I wasn't ready for sleep. Since I couldn't very well spend the night shuttling from one restaurant to another, I went to the office, and just as Toni had described it, the lobby guard had taken the night elevator down to the basement. I had no choice but to take the stairs.

I was still several floors below mine when I heard the piggy squeal of our hall door closing. I froze, my hand on the rail, and tried to tell myself it was nothing but my overwrought imagination. But it wasn't. There was no mistaking that sound. I looked at my watch. It was just after one o'clock. I slipped off my shoes and climbed slowly, warily, the treads gritty beneath my stockinged feet. When I reached the squeaky door I pushed it open with such glacial slowness that it didn't make a sound. Cautiously, I put my head through, looking first one way, then the other. The darkened hallway was absolutely still. As quiet as a tomb, I thought, and wished I hadn't.

Through the narrow opening I had so soundlessly made I insinuated myself into the hallway and stood absolutely dead still. Around the bend of the corridor I thought I heard a scraping noise. As silently as smoke I crept over to the corner and peeked around it just in time to see Ben's office door close at the far end of the corridor. I waited, but the light did not go on. I tried to keep my breathing regular. I waited. Still no light. I crept on, halfway down the hall, as far as the alcove that held the watercooler. Feeling like a fool, I wedged myself in behind the cooler and waited and worried. Toni, it seemed, was right about one thing, anyway— it certainly looked as though Ben was up to something. But was it Ben? If Ben let himself into his own office, the first thing he'd do would be to turn on the light. The watercooler burbled and I jumped straight up into the air, my heart thudding in my chest like a pile driver.

Through the frosted glass panel of the office directly across from me—Paul's office—a light flickered, then went out. A pinpoint of light, a pearl of light. A pencil-flashlight? Then the door opened silently and a dark, shadowy figure drifted down the hall toward Ben's office, turned the knob, and slipped silently inside.

Light blazed suddenly through the glass of Ben's door. Silhouetted figures struggled like shadow puppets. I rushed down the hall, ready to burst through the door, but the scuffle stopped. I could hear voices, not words, just the drone of two very different voices: Ben's baritone and a high tenor. I knew the other voice from somewhere, but I couldn't quite place it. The tenor backed up against the door, and that's when I saw the clear silhouette of a gun. A pistol. A man who was clearly not Ben was holding a gun on him. The shadow puppet disappeared from the bright glass.

I flew to that door like an avenging angel. Knees trembling, I put my hand on the doorknob. It was colder than fear. I took a deep breath and slowly turned the knob until I felt the latch give in blessed silence. Pressing the door in just a fraction, I carefully released the latch. Crouching, I pushed the door open far enough to see into the room.

Ben sat behind the desk with his hands locked behind his head, while Grice, a gun pointed at the middle of Ben's chest, stood facing him, on the opposite side of the desk, his free hand resting on a pile of manuscripts. Grice's back was to me and no more than a dozen feet away. Had Grice caught Ben, or had Ben caught Grice?

"You're a fool, Grice," Ben said. "You'll never get away with this."

Grice snorted. "You may be a crime editor, Malloy, but you don't know squat about the real world."

Holding my breath, I oozed through the door feeling as conspicuous as a balloon in the Macy's parade.

Ben must have seen me, but he didn't turn a hair. He never took his eyes off Grice. Now that I was in there, I didn't know what to do—the folly of not planning ahead. I doubted that I'd be very successful if I tried to throttle Grice.

Ben said, "Do you mean you think you can kill me and get away with it?"

"What's another murder in this city? Some poor slob of an editor is found shot at his desk . . ."

That's when I remembered the bookcase beside the door and its looming statuette.

". . .his wallet empty on the floor. Drugs. That's what everyone will assume . . ."

The Maltese Falcon was so heavy I nearly dropped it. I grabbed the bird by the neck with both hands and positioned myself behind Grice.

"Mugged, they'll say. Murdered by some spaced-out doper who robbed you to buy drugs, they'll say. Malloy, this little operation of Pomfret's is a gold mine. Did you know that? You editors with your heads in the sky, what do you know? By the time they carry you out in a body-bag Pomfret will be falling all over himself to sell this company. We're going to be right there to make him a very nice offer—you can be sure of that."

What if, by hitting Grice on the head, I caused a reflex spasm, and he emptied his gun into Ben's chest? What if . . . ? What if . . . ? My mind was a chaos of horrific images all ending with Ben dead, a great gaping hole in his chest. I raised the bird above my head.

Ben must have read my thoughts, because at that moment his head jerked up, his jaw fell open and he gaped at the ceiling as though a trapdoor had fallen open.

"Hey!" said Ben, his eyes on the ceiling.

Grice looked up, too, and the gun followed his glance.

I closed my eyes, said a prayer to my farm-grandmother who used to split kindling with an ax, and swung for all I was worth. I didn't hit him squarely. I missed his head completely and hit him on the shoulder, but it made the most awful sound, and he crumpled to the floor, swearing and moaning.

"You've broken his collarbone," said Ben who was straddling him in a flash. He tied Grice's hands with his own necktie and bound his feet with his belt. Grice lay with his eyes shut, whimpering. Ben pocketed the gun.

Only then did he take me in his arms, hugging me fiercely. "You've saved my life."

"Editorial prerogative, darling. I prefer happy endings. Hold me tighter, I'm still shaking."

"How did you know I'd be here?"

There were two possible answers to that question. One was dumb luck. I said, "Lover's intuition. Do you want to tell me what this is all about?"

"When all the odd things began happening around here, Mr. Pomfret asked me to find out who was behind it. He didn't want to call the police—you know how he is about publicity. So, I poked around, kept my ears and eyes open, staked out the office at night."

"Ah, ha!"

"What do you mean, 'Ah, ha!'?"

"Then it was you Toni saw going into Paul's office."

"Toni saw me? I was waiting for our Mr. X., but he didn't show. I was pretty sure by then that it was Grice who was sabotaging the Press. And I knew why. He was trying to terrorize Pomfret into giving up on the Press, washing his hands of the whole operation and selling it. But I couldn't prove it. It was only a couple of days ago that Mr. Pomfret learned Glactic Communications had been cheering Grice on from the sidelines, and waving bags of money at him to encourage him to sell."

"Who really called you back from France?"

"Pomfret got it into his head that Mr. X. was going to strike again, and he wanted me back in New York to catch him in the act."

"Why didn't you tell me?"

"I gave Pomfret my word."

"And you're a man of your word."

"Yes, Liz, I am, for better or for worse."

Ben hugged me to him with one arm. With his free hand he picked up the phone and called Pomfret. "We've got him," he said into the phone. He smiled at me over the receiver, listening, then he put his hand over the mouthpiece. "He wants to know who 'we' are," he said. "Liz Crosby and I, sir. We're a team." He kissed the top of my head. "How? Liz did it, sir. She put Grice out of commission. She slugged him with my Maltese Falcon . . . Yes, sir . . . Sometimes truth *is* stranger than fiction."

17

I STAND ON THE ROOF watching the sun slide like a ripe peach into Hoboken across the river. Ben is downstairs trying to persuade the caterer's man to go home and sleep it off. For some mysterious reason only Ben understands, inheriting the lease on Natasha Fleer's loft meant also inheriting her caterer. Natasha, buoyed by the enormous commercial success of her sculpture, has bought a farmhouse in Tuscany to be near a famous bronze foundry. And Ben, as a longtime favorite of hers, was offered first refusal on her studio-loft, which of course is far too large for one person to live in alone. I'm happy to say he had the very good sense to ask me what he should do.

It didn't take much to turn the loft from a "machine for living" into something resembling a comfortable home. In some areas we broke up the flow by putting up solid walls to create rooms where there had been only open space; in other areas we used freestanding bookcases as walls, and of course we put in a fireplace. A huge fireplace. And I'm proud to say that in all the remodeling, the only disagreement we had was over the equitable distribution of the shelves in the bathroom. I think that must be some sort of record.

THE CEREMONY WAS SIMPLE. Didn't I mention we got married? It must be the champagne. And very good champagne it is, too. Vintage. Provided by the ever-generous Mr. Pomfret. They're both downstairs, the Pomfrets. Hadley Pomfret is dancing with Chris, and his bother Harold is clasping Gudrun to his portly chest as though she were an equity distribution. As Gudrun is fully two heads taller than he, his face is squashed against her cleavage. From the smile on his face I suspect he is falling in love.

But I was talking about the wedding. It was very small—intimate, really, and very fast—in judge's chambers. I just happen to know this terrific judge, and she owed me a favor because I wrote a letter recommending her daughter for a summer internship at a publisher's. Ross and Toni stood up for us, and then we came back here for a combined wedding breakfast and housewarming. It's been going on for hours and hours and hours. Toni gave us a hand-carved dough-bowl. Ross gave us his jade plant. Everyone's been so generous. Ben says we have enough shrimp forks to serve seafood cocktail to the entire Swiss army.

I am smiling—quite giddy with happiness—into the waning sunset when I hear Toni's steps crossing the roof. I couldn't be seriously angry with Toni; it would be too schizophrenic—like being angry with myself. Besides, how can you stay angry at someone who can remember a semester when you were so depressed you ate nothing but Fig Newtons and blew up as big as the Goodyear Blimp and has never, ever told a living soul?

"Hi! Do you want company, or do you want to be alone?" she asked, obviously a little tipsy. "The bride is not supposed to brood on her wedding day, you know. It not considered tradi...tradi...It's not the usual thing. Here, have some more champagne, I've brought a fresh bottle. Ross just popped the cork for me."

"Did you see that jade plant?" I say. "It looks like Audrey Two in *The Little Shop of Horrors*. What do you suppose he feeds it?"

"Virgins. Did I tell you he was right about that Hepburn movie. I looked it up. Why didn't you ever tell me Ross is a closet opera nut?"

"Probably because I never knew. Isn't that what it means to be—?"

"He has friends at the Met. Isn't that incredible? On the production side. He told me he can be a super anytime he wants to. I was just trying to imagine what that must be like, when he asked me if I'd like to be a super in *Aida*."

"You mean walk on as an extra? Would you? Can you see yourself covered with brown body paint pretending to be a prisoner?"

"I said to Ross . . ." She sways a bit tipsily. "I said, 'Ross, I'll do it, if you'll do it.'" Her eyes glitter impishly. "We're going to do it! Me and Pavarotti on the same stage . . ." We sip our wine in companionable silence until Toni says, "Chris asked me if I'd like someone to share the apartment, but I said no. I felt like I'd finally grown up when I said it. It's an odd feeling. Funny thing is, I don't mind it at all."

We lean our elbows on the top of the parapet and watch the lights winking on in New Jersey.

"Look at that sky!" Toni says. "Have you ever seen such a glorious sky?"

"It'll be dark soon."

"Where's the wine?"

"Almost gone," I say. "Might as well finish it off."

"There's one thing I want you to know."

"Wazzat?"

"You may be Mrs. Malloy. . .Mrs. Ben Malloy. . ."

"Mrs. Benedict Thomas Malloy. . ."

". . .but you're still my Lizzie. And there'll always be a light on in my window for you."

"And mine for you. This doesn't change us, not you and me. Nothing could change what we have, not ever."

"I'll drink to that."

"A toast!" I raise my glass. "We must have a proper toast."

"To us!" says Toni.

"To us!"

We drain our glasses and, laughing, fling them high into the air. They soar away, two crystal birds catching fire from the setting sun—glinting red, glinting orange, twinkling crystal birds racing high and free, until they seem to shiver, hesitate, tumble over and plummet earthward. Linking arms we turn away toward the stairs, toward Ben, toward Ross. From far below, like distant music, rises the faint pure tinkling of breaking crystal, and we smile, just a little tearfully.

HARLEQUIN
American Romance®

THE ROMANCE THAT STARTED IT ALL!

For Diane Bauer and Nick Granatelli, the walk down the aisle was a rocky road....

Don't miss the romantic prequel to WITH THIS RING—

I THEE WED
BY ANNE McALLISTER

Harlequin American Romance #387

Let Anne McAllister take you to Cambridge, Massachusetts, to the night when an innocent blind date brought a reluctant Diane Bauer and Nick Granatelli together. For Diane, a smoldering attraction like theirs had only one fate, one future—marriage. The hard part, she learned, was convincing her intended....

Watch for Anne McAllister's I THEE WED, available *now* from Harlequin American Romance.

ITW

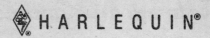

HARLEQUIN
Temptation

Lovers Apart

FOUR CONTROVERSIAL STORIES! FOUR DYNAMITE AUTHORS!

Don't miss the last book in the LOVERS APART miniseries, April's Temptation title #344, YOUR PLACE OR MINE by Vicki Lewis Thompson.